CELIA BUC

VILLAGE

CELIA Buckmaster was born on 28 November 1914, and her youth was spent in London and Buckinghamshire.

In September 1937 she married Robert Gibson-Fleming, but they divorced two years later. Around this time Celia Buckmaster moved in the London literary circles centring on Dylan Thomas, publishing work in progressive literary magazines. She was also close to poet Lynette Roberts, with whom she worked as a professional flower arranger.

In late 1939 Celia Buckmaster travelled to Burma and married Edmund Leach there in February 1940. In 1942, after the Japanese invasion of Burma, Celia returned to England with her new-born baby Loulou, and bought a house in the Hertfordshire village of Holwell. Celia and Edmund later had a son, Alexander, in 1946. The family moved to Cambridge in 1953 where Edmund Leach was a university lecturer. At Holwell Celia wrote her only two published novels, *Village Story* (1951) and *Family Ties* (1952).

Edmund Leach was knighted in 1975 and after his retirement the couple lived at Barrington, outside Cambridge. Lady Celia Leach died in 2005.

FICTION BY CELIA BUCKMASTER

Village Story (1951)

Family Ties (1952)

CELIA BUCKMASTER

VILLAGE STORY

With an introduction by
Elizabeth Crawford

DEAN STREET PRESS

A Furrowed Middlebrow Book
FM51

Published by Dean Street Press 2020

First published in 1951 by Hogarth Press

Cover by DSP

ISBN 978 1 913527 29 7

www.deanstreetpress.co.uk

Introduction

ON ITS publication in the summer of 1951 Celia Buck-master's *Village Story* prompted a response from reviewers that would have gratified any tyro novelist. Writing in *The Listener* (12 July 1951) John Russell commented, 'It is from *Between the Acts* that *Village Story* is unpretentiously descended' . . . [her] 'method is Vulpine', the author keeping 'events in their place; it is through the trellises of conversation that we glimpse them. Her own tone, too, is conversational; and its deceptive ease is the mark of a writer whose ear, alike for sentence structure and for the ring of colloquial speech, is exceptionally fine'. In the *Sunday Times* (17 June 1951) C.P. Snow praised Celia's ability to focus on 'the extreme delicacies of social gradation' when writing about 'the comfortably-off in the modern village', describing 'her pictures' as sharp-edged', and the novel at its best 'when Miss Buckmaster lets us see her claws'.

Celia Buckmaster published only one more novel, *Family Ties*, both issued by the Hogarth Press, the publishing house created by Leonard and Virginia Woolf. Although by 1951 the firm had been subsumed into Chatto and Windus, Leonard Woolf, whom Celia met and liked, was still a board member. Celia's daughter, Loulou Brown, believes that her mother was, as reviewers suggested, likely to have been inspired by the writing of Virginia Woolf and that the novels of Nancy Mitford, in which she took particular delight, were a possible other influence.

The milieu of Celia Buckmaster's upbringing was, however, neither that of the Bloomsbury intelligentsia nor of the county aristocracy. She was born on 28 November 1914, the eldest child of Guy Buckmaster (1886-1937) and his wife Barbara (*née* Geidt, 1888-1975). Her grandfather, Henry Buckmaster, was a brewer and Guy, when he married, was a manager in the family business. This was not a station in society favoured by his wife's family and by 1915 he had qualified as a barrister. The change of career could have been prompted by a desire to remove the taint of trade, anathema to the Geidts, but, more practically, was probably taken in the knowledge that the future of the family business was insecure; his father was made bankrupt in 1921. Celia's mother had been born and brought up in Germany, of British/Tasmanian parentage, very conscious of the wealth and social position that previous generations of the family had enjoyed.

Details of Celia Buckmaster's early years are shrouded in mystery; for instance, she never revealed to her daughter where and how she was educated or where, in detail, she lived as a child. Research reveals that in the 1920s and 1930s the family occupied a succession of houses in Northwood, on London's northern fringes, and then in Buckinghamshire. For many years they also had a London apartment in New Court, Carey Street, and, after Guy's death, his widow and children occupied a flat in King's Bench Walk, in the Temple.

Celia was close to none of her three siblings, although did her duty when necessary by her somewhat difficult sister. Loulou Brown remembers that she never wanted to talk about her relations, excepting only her uncle Maurice Buckmaster, who during the Second World War was head of the French Section of the SOE, was interviewed for the 1969 documentary, *Le Chagrin et la Pitié*, and can still be seen, playing himself, in the film *Odette*.

Guy Buckmaster died in March 1937 and in August Celia's engagement was announced to Robert Gibson-Fleming, a solicitor. The wedding took place in Kensington the following month. The marriage, however, proved disastrous and two years later Celia, still only 24 years old, emerged from it, a divorced woman. As such she incurred severe disapproval from some family members and in later years knowledge of this first marriage was firmly suppressed. Traumatised, she took to her bed, only emerging after treatment, found for her by her mother, from Kilton Stewart, an unconventional US psychotherapist. The retelling of dreams, a feature of *Village Story*, may be a nod to Stewart's work on dream theory.

In the late 1930s Celia Buckmaster moved in the London circle that centred on Dylan Thomas, publishing work in a handful of progressive literary magazines, such as *Wales*, *Seven*, *Twentieth Century Verse*, and *Poetry: London*. She was particularly close to the poet Lynette Roberts, acting as bridesmaid at her wedding in October 1939, her beauty remarked by the best man, Dylan Thomas. A few days earlier, when supplying information to the enumerator of the 1939 Register, Celia described herself as a 'Flower Decorator', for, with Lynette Roberts, she operated a rather bohemian little business, 'Bruska', buying flowers from Covent Garden and arranging them in the homes of the wealthy. In late 1938 and early 1939 the two young women had spent a couple of months in Madeira, their journey home enlivened by a near ship-wreck. Celia, described as 'poet and authoress', was reported by the *Daily Mail* (10 April 1939) to be worried about the fate of 'the novel she was writing [and] pictures she had painted'. For Celia was indeed an artist, flowers her subjects of choice. She appears to have had no formal training other than that gained during post-war annual visits to the Suffolk art school run at Benton End by Cedric Morris and Arthur Lett-Haines. These visits gave her the utmost pleasure. It is no stretch of the imagination to find elements of Celia in Eileen Noyce, the artist at the heart of *Village Story*. At the most material level, Celia, like Eileen, wore and loved a red cloak, most suitable attire for an artist, hers a present from Lynette Roberts. Like Eileen, Celia was to exhibit her paintings on at least one occasion.

In late 1939 Celia Buckmaster travelled to Burma to marry Edmund Leach, later an eminent anthropologist, the wedding taking place in Rangoon (Yangon) the day after her arrival in February 1940. They had been introduced by Kilton Stewart, with whom Leach had a few years earlier undertaken his first, still amateur, fieldwork on an island off Formosa [Taiwan]. Loulou Brown acknowledges that, as 'Mr Swan' in *Family Ties* had returned from the East with the idea of finding a wife, so a faint parallel could be drawn with the inception of her parent's marriage. In 1942, after the Japanese invasion of Burma, Celia, carrying her baby, Loulou, made a hazardous journey back to England, where she eventually bought a dilapidated, part-Elizabethan house, 'Gurneys', in the Hertfordshire village of Holwell. After the War the family, augmented by the birth of a son, Alexander, in 1946, continued living at Holwell until moving to Cambridge in 1953 following Leach's appointment as a university lecturer. It was in Holwell that Celia wrote her two published novels. Leach was knighted in 1975 and after his retirement as provost of King's College in 1979 the couple lived at Barrington, outside Cambridge. Lady Celia Leach died in 2005.

Elizabeth Crawford

CHAPTER ONE

IN A village a new face is new for a very long time, and a new name remains strange until it is put on a tombstone and so becomes one of the family at last. Apart from this, village life is much the same as any other sort of life; hard work, the struggle to make ends meet, strokes of luck, sudden catastrophes—most people have to deal with these. Some change with their changing lot to become cantankerous, vain or resigned, as things may be, while others remain true to some strain in themselves which carries them along fighting to the end. The people I am going to tell you about are quite ordinary. They would agree that things could be very much better, and some make rather a fuss, while others do not. No one starves in this particular village, so my story is not the painful sort that deals with food, warmth and shelter (the realities), but rather with the worries that afflict people who are comfortably off; though they themselves would be the first to tell you how ruinous taxation is and how the Government has bled them white of all their money.

But first I want to describe the family who live in the cottage with the nicest garden in the village. All the villagers take pride in their gardens, and all the gardens are pleasant and tidy, but Mr. Darlington's was the best. He loved roses, and at the end of many years of hard work at the local Manor, he retired with a small pension to grow roses for his own pleasure. His wife brought in a little extra money by helping in families with new-born babies and laying-out corpses, but his daughter, who was said to be "gifted" by one of her teachers (a lady who came from the town twice a month to teach music), had now left school and did no work. People who have gifts above the average are sometimes made to suffer in a community like a village, but it would be hard to tell in what way this girl differed from anyone else, except that she was very spoilt and very pretty. She hung about the place, not helping much and spending a lot of time over her appearance, more even than is usual with a pretty girl. At last the irritated mother could bear it no longer. She took her daughter to the Manor, where her father had worked before her, and, through the cook there, got her taken on as maid-of-all-work. The cook was a village woman known as Mrs. Walmby, which was a courtesy title, for she was really only Miss, who had quarrelled with her brother when he married, and left his house to go and live at the Manor, where she had worked ever since. Now, unlike the old days when the old master and mistress had lived there, the Manor-house was almost empty, and Mrs. Walmby and an old family nurse were the only servants left to look after the new Mr. and Mrs. Noyce, who had come there to live. So it was lonely.

Mrs. Walmby and the old nurse always had tea together at about eleven o'clock, while Linda (Mrs. Darlington's daughter) was supposed to have hers sitting at the kitchen table after Mrs. Walmby had poured out a cup for her and gone off to join nurse. But one day in a fit of bad temper Linda said that she did not want any tea. Mrs. Walmby pursed her lips, poured it out just the same, and went off to tell nurse. Linda went out into the garden. It was a lovely day, and Mr. Noyce sat under a chestnut-tree reading André Gide. He looked up from his book casually, as though his thoughts were straying, and he saw a pretty girl coming along the path between the roses towards him. He smiled. Linda said "Good morning," and took a turn to the left. But after this she began taking even more trouble with her appearance, and smiled when people asked her how she was getting on up at the Manor, and said little but dropped hints.

Mr. Noyce was no Squire of the village with a Squire's idea of importance. The village accepted his presence; he was there because his father had been there, and his small estate was managed by the families living in the tied cottages. They were safe enough there; Mr. Noyce would never evict them, because if he did no one would work for him. He had no positive influence on village life. When they noticed the girl's behaviour and saw what she was getting at, most people, and especially her neighbours who had suffered her airs and graces from childhood, thought Linda was daft.

But Mr. Noyce is still smiling in the garden. More likely he smiles from his inner world, not at the world outside him, though he did see the girl in the garden, and if it had been his wife coming towards him, he would not have smiled. He brought a note-book and pencil out of his pocket when Linda turned off the path away from him, and wrote down, still smiling:

"Tuesday, September 2nd. Dreamed I saw the Dancer in the garden. This morning saw a girl walking towards me while I read under the old chestnut. Prevision? Must remember to . . ."

At that moment a window opened in the top storey of the house and a voice called out "Harry!" He frowned and finished off the sentence quickly:

". . . write down my dreams as I wake in the morning."

and closed the book and put it away in his pocket with the pencil.

"What's the matter?" he called out. "Oh, all right. Don't shout. I'm coming."

His wife watched him from the window. She was an artist, and had just finished painting a picture. And now she had nothing to do. She closed the window and waited for her husband.

"What about that party?" she said when he came in. "You're always saying we ought to give a party. Well, I thought of asking them all up one day fairly soon. If you give me some wine, I'll make it a real dinner. What do you think?" She picked up a piece of paper from the table and checked off a number of names on her fingers. "Eight with us," she said. "If Mr. Browning's mother goes out, that is."

When she spoke about asking them all up, she did not mean the whole village, nor even her friends. She meant the people who lived in the three other big houses in the village. She had no friends.

"I suppose we really ought to," Mr. Noyce said. He loved parties, but not that sort. He liked London parties, cosmopolitan affairs; but these had vanished from his life when about a year ago, at the age of fifty, he had inherited his father's estate and come to live in the country.

"Yes, yes," he said now. (He was looking at the picture his wife had just finished painting.) "I think I see what you mean, my dear. But as I said before, I still think that green a little too obvious. But perhaps obvious isn't the right word for what I mean."

"Don't let's bother about that now," his wife said.

He saw the look on her face.

"I'm sorry. I shouldn't have spoken, I suppose," he said, "but what did you call me all the way up here for, then?"

She did not answer, and dropped the list of names on the floor and turned her back on both her husband and her painting and stared in silence out of the window. Mr. Noyce, who did not love her any more, came over and patted her on the shoulder.

"All right, all right, my dear, you shall have your party," he said.

But it is Mrs. Ethelburger and her husband who are interesting, not Mr. and Mrs. Noyce. Mr. Ethelburger is a gentleman farmer. He is not rich, and any money he makes is put back again into the farm, so the furniture in his home is all old-fashioned and most of the rooms need painting. But there is always plenty of food on his table, and his four children, who make a great deal of noise, are good-looking, healthy children. Mrs. Ethelburger is the heroine of this story. Something is always happening on a farm—calves are being born, geese gaggle in the middle of the night as a fox gets in at the chickens, a cloudburst flattens the corn at harvest-time, and, besides, meals have to be ready at odd times to suit the men, so that it is not an easy thing to be a farmer's wife. Of course, if Mrs. Ethelburger had been efficient and house-proud it might have been a bit easier. The house was very badly run. There was a lot of waste; cream often went sour, lights were left on in the kitchen all night, the cats helped themselves in the larder. A girl called Irene came up from the village to help in the house, but sometimes, because Mrs. Ethelburger had forgotten to give her anything to do, she would stare out of the kitchen window for hours at a time with her elbows on the sink. She was not an intelligent girl, and was happy like that. Mrs. Ethelburger, who sat down when she wanted to think, had been classed as very intelligent when a girl, but seeing her in this ramshackle house, surrounded by her noisy family (as though there were not enough children about, there were photos of them all over the mantelpiece), people had wondered: hadn't she rather thrown herself away? She was still lovely, but there were lines on her face. Hadn't she really let her mind go to seed in this place? Need she be quite so vague, so untidy? What on earth went on in her head all day? These were the sort of questions her relatives, paying a visit, asked themselves. Nobody stayed very long at the farm, it was too uncomfortable. It was all right for men who were out all day and came back longing for a good meal and then sleep, but there was nothing feminine about the house that suggested grace and leisure, and the pictures and the furniture and the whole arrangement of the place gave no positive indication whatsoever of Mrs. Ethelburger's character. She was a tall, fair woman with large eyes that looked hard at people so that they felt inclined to keep their distance; and this suited her very well because, although she was interested in people at first, she soon grew tired of them. Her children had interested her once when they were small and helpless, but now that they were growing up they ceased to claim her attention, except in so far as she was bound to wash and feed them. She worked with spasmodic energy in the house, was a good but erratic cook, and when there was nothing urgent to be done about the place, sat about day-dreaming. This annoyed Mr. Ethelburger, who said: "Can't you find anything better to do than sit about all day? I really can't run this place by myself."

But they were fond of one another just the same.

"Don't forget to answer the Noyces' invitation," said Mr. Ethelburger to his wife one day. "We'd better go. It would do you good to get out for a bit."

The invitation lay about on the mantelpiece for a few days more till Mr. Ethelburger, tired of seeing it, answered it himself and propped the addressed envelope up against an empty flower-pot in the hall. Mrs. Ethelburger saw it there after lunch. It had no stamp on, and as it was as much trouble to walk down to the post-office as to walk through the orchard to the Manor, she decided to make up for her laziness and take the answer up to the Noyces herself. The orchard belonged to Mr. Noyce. He had had notices put up saying 'Private Property.' But Mrs. Ethelburger did not bother about these and climbed through the fence. She had been a friend of old Mr. Noyce, whom she had often visited. Her own home had been very much like the Manor, and she had loved the old man as unaffectedly as a child, while he had come to look upon her, with some amusement, as a daughter. But since he died, Mrs. Ethelburger had only once, and then for the sake of courtesy, visited the Manor. Walking slowly up the drive towards the house, she looked about her for alterations or improvements, but there were none. She smiled, slipping back to the day-dreams of her own childhood, unchanged.

Mr. Noyce, who was enjoying himself in the old nurse's parlour, teasing her about religion (she was a Baptist; he had no religion at all), saw Mrs. Ethelburger dawdling along up the drive through the window.

"Who is the stray goddess coming to visit us?" he said, waving aside a cloud of cigarette smoke the better to see. The old nurse stopped turning the handle of her sewing-machine and laid her hand on the wheel so that it came to a stop. She peered out of the window directly in front of her.

"That's Barbara Ethelburger," she said. "Your father was very fond of her. There's no reason why you shouldn't be friends with her yourself."

"Rather a forbidding type of person," Mr. Noyce said. "I remember when she called here and left her card, or whatever it is they still do in the country."

"There's no harm to her. She's just a child," said the nurse.

"A spoilt child," Mr. Noyce said.

The old woman turned away from the window and looked at her master, who was still, now that he was back again in this house, her child. "Always judging others by yourself! It's the wrong way, Master Harry," she said.

"But the only way, Nurse," said Mr. Noyce. "I have only one medium of expression, only one criterion, only one source of inspiration, and that is the fearful muddle of instincts and intellect which I know as 'myself.' What you say about me, Nurse, is yourself to me when I am good enough to notice you; what you know about me is only 'myself' to you, if you really do exist. I suppose you must."

"It's no good your showing off like that to me," the old nurse said. "I've got work to do. You go along and entertain your visitor."

Meanwhile Mrs. Ethelburger had entered the house and Mrs. Noyce had been summoned from her studio upstairs to meet her. They shook hands. Mrs. Ethelburger's long fair hair fell about her face and shoulders, untidy as usual.

"I'm so sorry to disturb you," she said. "I needn't have even rung the bell, really. It's just this letter for you."

Mrs. Noyce took it from her. "Won't you sit down," she said coldly.

Just then Mr. Noyce came in. He, too, shook hands with Mrs. Ethelburger, but managed to put a little warmth in his greeting. He countered her hard stare with a look from his own non-committal eyes, and so they stood there, looking at each other rather longer than was polite. Suddenly Mrs. Ethelburger's eyes filled with tears.

"I was very fond of your father," she said. "I loved him so much."

Mr. Noyce turned away in confusion, and began searching in his pocket for a cigarette.

"But he was an old man," he said; "very, very old, you know."

Mrs. Noyce sprang forward from a chair she was leaning against, and, picking up a box of cigarettes from the table, almost pushed them in her husband's face.

"Here they are!" she said. "Don't take one first. Offer them to Mrs. Ethelburger. Didn't you know? She's an old friend of the family. She belongs here more than we do. She must come here often. Why hasn't she been up here before!"

In order to draw attention to herself, she began to chatter about anything that came into her head, but this only served to make the other two more interested in each other; they scarcely bothered to answer her. It was an unhappy conversation.

When Mrs. Ethelburger had gone, the husband and wife found it difficult to separate. Each had work to do; Mr. Noyce had an appointment with his bailiff that afternoon at half-past three, and it was past that time already, while Mrs. Noyce was eager to get on with a new painting. This obligation to work pressed on their minds, but at the same time both were aware of feelings which needed some form of expression. Neither would have chosen to speak to the other on such an occasion, but since they were alone together they had no choice.

"Fancy having four children," Mrs. Noyce said.

Mr. Noyce tapped his forefinger against the window-pane.

"She reminds me of someone," he said, "that face—you ought to paint her, Eileen."

"She doesn't interest me like that," Mrs. Noyce said. "Besides, I'm no good at portraits."

"How does one become interested, then? I should have thought those planes, that bone structure—no, what nonsense it all is! Just like mother all over again—'If I were a man, I'd do so and so'—If I were a painter, that's the sort of thing I'd paint. Be my life all over again instead of me. What a hope! Poor mother."

Mr. Noyce breathed heavily and clouded the window-pane.

"And poor me," his wife said.

"Quite right, quite right," he added at once. "But don't let's be sorry for you, if you don't mind. I really must get on. And so must you, I daresay. Mother never had enough to do, she always got headaches. You can put it all in a picture. How fortunate!"

"I told you, I'm not interested," Mrs. Noyce said.

He gave himself a little slap on the forehead.

"Now I've got it," he said. "Botticelli's *Primavera*! That's it. Spring. The one on the right-hand side, that's Mrs. Ethelburger. No, Eileen, don't paint her."

"I shouldn't dream of doing so," she said.

Mr. Noyce fingered the little book in his pocket, and was just about to say something about dreams when he saw the bailiff coming up a path towards the house.

"Oh, Lord, you women—what time-wasters you all are," he said. "Now I shall have to make some fantastic excuse to Broom, and he thinks I'm an old fool, anyway."

"Just like a man!" burst out Mrs. Noyce. "Selfish and hard, and always putting the blame on someone else. Who's been wasting my time, I should like to know? If your father's friends choose to call, it's I who have to see them, not you. And don't forget either, there's no fool like an old fool."

They glared at one another, hostile and trembling.

Mr. Noyce controlled the words of violence and aggression that flew up into his brain, closing his mouth on them, living them in silence.

Mr. Broom knocked on the french windows.

"How dare you!" cried out Mr. Noyce. "Go and wait by the big barn. I said I'd meet you there, didn't I?"

To Mr. Broom outside, peering in through the window, it seemed a comfortable room to be in; big chairs, a sofa long enough to put one's feet up on. He wondered why they stood about, since obviously they lived a sort of parlour existence.

"All right, all right, Mr. Noyce, you just take your time," he said. He didn't want to be annoyed that afternoon. He had a plan for the apple orchard, and also a contract which he intended his master should sign. And he very well knew that after such a show of bad temper Mr. Noyce would be exceptionally calm. To assert his indifference (he disliked waiting about), he lingered at the window before turning away, and so got a glimpse of the kind of life that went on in that comfortable room. Mrs. Noyce picked up a little silver object from the table and threw it at her husband. Mr. Broom had turned away as it came whirling from her hand, and did not look round to see whether she had hit or missed. He heard the window break just behind him, but went away down the path as though nothing had happened.

"Bitch," he said. "They're all the same." His own wife was childless, and he had come to the conclusion that barrenness was the root of all evil. A kind man with a sad look in his eyes, he would never, in fact, have laid hands on his wife with intent to harm her, but noticing how she treated animals, giving the dog a kick when she stumbled over him in the dark, shouting abuse at the proud geese when they invaded her garden, he had sometimes longed to beat her with the little whip she kept to train the cats. Besides having no children, Mrs. Broom and Mrs. Noyce had other things in common. Mrs. Broom had belonged to a circus before she married, and so to a certain extent had the feelings of a creative artist. She had been trained to do a small act with the lions; but one day there was an accident and her face was lacerated. Badly shaken and disfigured, she was no good for the circus any more. She then married Mr. Broom, who had always been after her (he had met her in the town near the village when first the circus came there, and then they had exchanged letters, meeting seldom but being faithful to each other), and now, perhaps out of nostalgia for the circus, she trained cats to do little tricks, such as jumping over boxes and leaping at her when she called. This ruined her temper, because cats are so hard to train. She had one friend, the village post-mistress—a large, domineering woman like herself, who lived in almost perfect peace with a frail, domesticated husband and two grown-up boys who went away to work. The post-mistress, Mrs. Blonsom, was on friendly terms with Mrs. Ethelburger. Both women kept bees, and when the time came for honey to be extracted, they helped each other. At Christmas they exchanged presents, and at all times of the year were glad to meet and have a talk. They did not exactly gossip, but were inclined to shake their heads together over the frailties of human nature.

Coming up the drive with the afternoon post, Mr. Blonsom met Mr. Broom, who was shuffling along looking sad.

"Nice day," Mr. Blonsom said.

"For some," said Mr. Broom.

"Why, anything wrong?"

Mr. Broom pointed his thumb backwards over his shoulder and winked.

"We're not the only ones, my lad, you and me, to have a spot of trouble with the missus," he said.

Mr. Blonsom took his foot off the pedal and held the bicycle steady by the handlebars.

"Go on!" he said. "What's the trouble, then?"

But Mr. Broom was no talker, and, having shown he knew a thing or two, was not going to give away secrets. He whistled and moved on. Had it been anyone else but Mr. Blonsom, he might never have spoken of what he had seen, but nursed it to himself, adding to the burden of spite against womanhood he carried with him. He considered Mr. Blonsom to be a harmless, foolish man, and he had been unable to resist the temptation of showing off a little.

Mischievous words such as these can work like poison in the mind. Mr. Blonsom, outwardly so kind, so gentle, was also a coward and mean. None knew this better than his wife, who both sheltered and repressed him. But you cannot altogether harness a man's tongue. Men have other interests than women, and talk about spreading news rather than gossip, because news is more important than gossip and men are always more important than women. But Mr. Blonsom, tied to his wife's apron-strings, had become infected with women's tittle-tattle, not because Mrs. Blonsom herself let her tongue wag, but simply from playing second fiddle all his life, not being allowed to do things, being unimportant, doing the necessary odd jobs which fall to the lesser one of any partnership.

"How awkward life is with a woman," wrote Mr. Noyce in his diary that evening. "Culture is skin deep with them, I begin to see, and does not grow from within. And yet, shall I always be able to control myself? Perhaps I am just a suave, thinking brute more cruel than any woman. To-day E. threw mother's little christening-cup at me, the rather austere George III one. Dented between the handles—and no wonder, as it broke the window! Curious. Did she want to wound me (in two senses!) by using something for that purpose that she knew I held in affection, or would anything have done in that moment of blind rage? She chose the christening-cup out of so many things, it could hardly have been fate. But nurse says she sometimes breaks things when she's washing-up 'because the Devil must have tempted her when she was tired and didn't want to do it.' One can see the unconscious workings of the mind there all right—to hell with all this nonsense: break it, and then you won't have to do it! And so, the accident. I had been talking about my mother. Why do women hate each other? I'm sure E. simply loathed our visitor. Jealous for these reasons: (i) because Mrs. E. has four children and she has none; (ii) because I obviously showed interest; and (iii) because she feels drawn to our visitor herself—I sensed that at once. But how irrational! E. has always accused me of lack of interest in other people ('You are only interested in yourself, that's why we have no friends,' etc., etc.). And being drawn to the woman, why at once repel her because I happened to be drawn also? Sometimes I think her mind is quite 'housemaid.' Doesn't she know me well enough to trust me with women by this time? Perhaps painting for her is a sort of twisting of the impulses, a too-small channel carved for the diverted main stream of her sexual and maternal loves. Her soul is flooded. But if only she will go on working at it, one day she will paint. Personalities, egos—what a nuisance they are! Top-layer façades, how they get in the way. Always trying to be a Someone when one can only be one's self. And how E. offends herself by trying to be someone else. Or perhaps I don't know who she is, or she is no one. An all-round unsatisfactory creature, the artist as a woman. *Memo. . . .*"

There was a knock on the door just then. Mr. Noyce took off his glasses and said, "Come in."

It was Linda. She came right into the room and closed the door behind her. "Can I post any letters for you, or anything? I'm just off home," she said.

Mr. Noyce frowned. "Certainly not," he said. "Who told you to come in here? Don't you know, I dislike being disturbed? Don't do it again." He turned away from her, and was just picking up his glasses when she said, "It was my own idea. I like helping."

He turned towards her again. "Now go away," he said. "You're the little girl from the village, aren't you? Well, I don't want to be cross with you. It's nice of you to want to help, but, you see, your job is in the kitchen. Perhaps you don't find that very interesting—you want to better yourself. Well, if you are intelligent, you can learn a great deal from Mrs. Walmby; she's a good cook. That's how you can help. But you are wasting my time, you see."

"Thank you, Sir," said Linda. "I'm sorry. I won't come in here again."

After she had gone, Mr. Noyce continued to look at the place in the room, about half-way between himself and the door, where she had stood.

"She's proud," he said to himself. "I've hurt her feelings." He tried to remember what it felt like to be young. "It was the uncertainty, the terror of being made to look ridiculous that was so awful," he said. Then he put on his glasses again. But for the life of him he could not remember what that important *Memo* was to be. At last he wrote down very quickly: "Must pay nurse's wages," blotted the whole page vigorously, and closed the book.

And nurse, whom you probably think of as a minor character, a subdued joke, as it were, is an important person really. Her kind is dying out, but once people like her formed the infant minds of the country's rulers. Upper-class families, whose sons were destined to pass through the Public Schools and then the appropriate Universities, and thence onward guiding the nation's affairs, all had nurses. These women, once so intimately bound up with affairs, we are inclined to think of now as old-fashioned, Old Testament creatures really. And Old Testament they are. A man of Mr. Noyce's age, if he had a nurse in infancy, most certainly has the voice of conscience somewhere among his inner voices. It speaks with rather a common voice perhaps, muttering the Ten Commandments, gives warning about punishment, and says "Now, now" in awkward situations. That is nurse. Naturally when conscience is outmoded, so is nurse. We laugh at her and tease like Mr. Noyce. But Mr. Noyce will always feel a little guilty. There are still nurses, of course, to this day, for any class that can afford them, admirable nurses, young and college trained, but their function has altered with the times. They are interested in diet—vitamins and so forth, and child psychology has opened up a whole new field of investigation for them; so that it is to science that they look for inspiration at their task, not religion. "Carrots make you see in the dark," the modern nurse might well say to the finicky feeder, but: "Think what you said at Grace, Master Harry, and eat what's put before you"—certainly not.

Old nurse spends her time now mending and sewing in her dusty parlour. She is growing blind, and besides her silver-rimmed spectacles, she must read the Bible in the evenings with the help of a magnifying-glass. The mice trouble her, she can hear them gnawing at the wainscoting, and so she keeps her large neutered cat Marcus constantly at her side. There is always a fire burning in her room and a black kettle singing on the hob. Her hands are twisted with arthritis so that if she points an accusing finger her hand will not obey her and she cannot stretch it out. She wears only boots now, they help her with her ankles, and these are nearly hidden under the skirts of her voluminous grey dresses. She always has a shawl on, but not an apron, and the large black hairpins, which she uses to keep up her masses of white hair, catch at the shawl at the back of her neck so that she feels the shawl slipping and hunches her shoulders. Her voice trembles a little when she speaks, like someone reading who knows the end of the sad story. She still trusts in the Lord.

Linda, smiling to herself, not looking where she was going, bumped into nurse by the green baize door which led down the passage-way into the kitchen.

"Be careful, my girl," nurse said, steadying herself against the wall.

"Sorry," said Linda. "I've just been to see whether Mr. Noyce had any letters for the post, and he kept me talking."

"Well now, it's a pity you're in such a hurry to be off," nurse said, "because there's something I've been wanting to talk to you about, myself. Just come along to my room for a moment, I won't keep you long."

Linda hesitated, but the old woman went on into the hall without looking back, and so she followed her.

It was warm and golden with the evening sun in nurse's room. The cat, whose dreaming amber eyes were all but closed, sat purring on the window-sill.

"Stand there where I can see you," nurse said.

Linda blinked in the sun, which, though not strong, was level with her eyes.

"Now, times may have changed," the old woman went on, "and it's not the same you working here as when your father worked for the old master. Girls don't know what service is; they don't know their place any more. It's hard for them; it must be hard all this struggling and pushing to better themselves, when in olden times they fitted in where there was room for them. But I'd have you know, my girl, we're content to let things be as they always were in this house."

"You're making trouble," said Linda. "You want to push me out."

"You'll go just as soon as the mistress tells you to go. Nobody's talking about dismissal now."

Nurse said this so gently that it was impossible for Linda to take offence; at any rate, not at the time of speaking.

"Well, what are you getting at, then?" she said. "You've been listening to talk."

"I can still hear what they're saying," nurse said.

"You shouldn't listen to gossip, then," said Linda.

The old woman sat down and folded her hands in her lap. "It's for your own good I'm speaking, never mind about other people's," she said. "Don't give yourself airs; that's where you spoil yourself, my child. And if you want to make a place for yourself here, it doesn't do to cross me."

"And it doesn't do to cross me either," Linda said. "I don't like being ordered about and threatened. And what have I done wrong, may I ask? It's because you think I get on too well with Mr. Noyce, you don't like me—isn't it? Well, perhaps we are friendly."

Nurse pulled her shawl round her and did not answer.

"I said, we are friendly," repeated Linda.

Just then Mr. Noyce came in. He had knocked on the door but had not waited for an answer.

"About money, Nurse; I won't keep you a moment," he said, and paused, waiting for Linda to go. But lifting her head she stood quite still, staring out of the window while the cat rubbed its ears against her arm.

"Your mother will be waiting. Run along now," said nurse gently.

Mr. Noyce stood with his back to the fire and looked up at the ceiling.

"I'll go; I know when I'm not wanted," Linda said. She walked quickly across the room and touched Mr. Noyce on the arm and, as he drew himself away, said, "Help me; they're all against me."

"I, really, I—perhaps my wife—" Mr. Noyce said. He leaned as far away from her as he could, and put one arm on nurse's chair to steady himself.

"Will you go now, please?" nurse said.

Linda was still crying when she got home. Her parents had long since finished their meal, and had left something for her by the fire. When she had eaten a little, her mother asked her if she would help with the ironing, but Linda said she was too tired, and went to bed. Her parents did not talk about her after she had gone, but started quarrelling about some trifle. Linda could hear them in her room above the kitchen.

It is dark now, and the owls have come out of their places of concealment. The Rector's wife goes into a little room on the second floor, where she has made a sanctuary for herself, and draws the curtains. She sits down at her bureau and looks through the bundles of papers stuffed in the pigeon-holes. There is nothing urgent for her to do, and so she gets out some large sheets of typing paper (notepaper is expensive and she keeps it locked away in the bottom drawer), and begins writing a letter to her sister.

"Dear Emm," she writes down, without bothering to put her address or the date at the top of the page:

"Dear Emm, you know what my life is like! It hasn't changed since you left, in fact, it's more the same—so you will understand my feelings when I tell you that we have been asked to dine at the Manor next week. I had thought of refusing, but Arthur said we must go as there was no plausible excuse for our refusal. As always, I see that he is right: we must go. So imagine me Saturday week in my black dress, feeling rather cold down the back I expect, talking to Mr. Noyce and trying not to feel depressed. All the 'Gentry' will be there, and Mr. Browning, too, will have had an invitation, and will probably come in case there are any influential people asked down from London. But I don't think he'll let his mother come. Don't go imagining I've changed my mind about Mr. Browning. I still like him immensely—in fact, I find myself counting on him for all sorts of advice, about the garden, about house repairs, about troubles in the village—all sorts of things that Arthur would naturally turn away from and that would fall to me as part of my work. And, anyway, you and I have always hated snobbery! It isn't that, Emm, it's the tireless egoism of the man that puts my back up. You know he's proud of his poor old mother, in a way; tells you how she was just a washerwoman before he made himself and raised her up; but when it's a question of any social function, bang, he drops her. It wouldn't do to have her dropping aitches in front of strangers. One realises, though, how hard it is for him always trying to get accepted, and just because of this I suppose he has had to make himself pushing and presumptuous. Do you know, he practically runs the service now? Reads the Lessons, chooses the hymns and even comments on the length of Arthur's sermons! This sort of lead should come from the Manor, as we all know, and as it isn't forthcoming, I suppose we should be grateful for interest shown in other quarters. But sometimes when he starts bullying Arthur with his 'you take it from me' and 'a Parson wouldn't know that'—it just makes me wild. If it wasn't that his betters obviously take not the slightest interest in the Church I should begin to wonder whether Arthur and I were not just another stepping-stone. But I must say, the man does care about his religion, which is more than can be said of most.

"This reminds me, do you remember my charlady, Mrs. White? The dark one with the long thin face with straight hair coming down to ear level? (We said she must have cut it with a bowl on!) Well, she came in with my tea one day in the middle of the morning and said, 'Do you think the next life's going to be any better than this one, Mrs. Spark?' Coming at me like that, I rather lost my head. 'Yes, it must be,' I said. 'That's what I say,' Mrs. White said. I try hard in the intervals of running this impossible house to interest myself in Mrs. W. and her troubles, but like the rest of them, I don't think she has really got anything to moan about. Emm dear, do you think I'm getting a hard woman? I know your loving heart will find excuses for me, but ever since Bob died, I feel a little contemptuous of all these people who moan and groan and make a fuss. And I have even begun to dislike the company of children. Oh, those dreadful Ethelburger children! But I am doing nothing but criticise. Forgive me. You see, I let myself go with you, and you get the nasty things which have been pent up all day. For all day long I must say sweetly, 'Dear Mrs. So-and-so, dear Mr. That.' How shall I ever become resigned to . . ."

She laid down her pen. "To what?" she said aloud. There were tears in her eyes, and she felt ashamed. She got up and, opening the door, stood listening a moment in the passage-way. Then she called out, "Coo-ee! Arthur! You all right, dear?"

"Quite all right," answered a muffled voice from downstairs.

"Don't get chilled, dear," Mrs. Spark said. "I'll be down in a minute. Just finishing Emm's letter." Sitting at her bureau once more, pen in hand, she tried to imagine her sister again; to talk to her as it were. But always the thought of her husband intervened. He was getting cold down there, or he was calling her (she listened), or she foresaw him look at her over the top of his glasses saying, "Read out the funny bits, dear—you're such a wit when you start writing letters."

And Emm wasn't there any more. She read through the letter.

"It'll just have to do as it is," she said. And crossing out the half-finished sentence at the end she wrote instead: "And now, dearest Emm, I must end here. Arthur calls me and I must go. With much love from your devoted sister—Clare."

It was still possible to read the crossed-out words, so she wrote 'apples' all over them.

CHAPTER TWO

ENERGETIC, wilful people always gather a little court of sycophants and followers about them, while their detractors, instead of keeping away as normally one keeps away from people one dislikes, are drawn towards them by the very strength of that dislike. Mr. Browning is not quite the person Mrs. Spark makes him out to be. "He's a one," they say, winking as he goes out of the pub. He is popular with the mediocrity, those who say a lot but don't do very much. The few violently discontented or over ambitious among the villagers hate him. He is, in fact, a very capable man; self-made, wise and humble where he cannot hope to excel. He is not married yet. Mr. Browning is a very interesting person indeed. It is quite untrue that he is ashamed about his mother dropping aitches. He drops them himself sometimes to show his mastery over such trifles, but without his mother he knows he would never have got very far. It is she who dislikes hobnobbing with narrow-minded people who distress themselves about aitches and so forth. She thinks a lot of her son, but is sad that ambition has made him so lonely. A washerwoman has a thousand contacts and is on equal terms with the majority, but the mother of a son who has made his way into a smaller society must sometimes feel regretful, both for herself and for him, that there is no one now to laugh with and make easy chatter, as there was for all in the old days. Mr. Browning is very much a local character. He knows and talks about gardening, plumbing, and of course the law (he is a solicitor), and anything relating to rates and taxes and so on. He loves birds, but never goes about shooting them. He is what Mrs. Spark calls 'sentimental' about animals.

It is Saturday, and he is reclining on a comfortable long wickerwork chair (the kind that has a little tray on two legs for the feet), passing the time of day with the Rector and a glass of sherry. They are on the south verandah of his house, where the Clematis Montana grows. This creeper has a sweet and lulling smell that suits evening time. Mr. Browning and Mr. Spark look out over the lawns towards the pond. Mr. Browning has turned the fountain on; they watch the water bubble out of the cornucopia to cream and fall, cream and fall. They meditate. I myself would never disturb such peace. But Barbara Ethelburger is coming down the drive.

"Drat the woman," Mr. Browning says.

Mrs. Ethelburger was very happy. She laid a bunch of large scarlet roses on the table by the sherry and said, "I'm sure your garden doesn't grow such perfect roses Mr. Browning." The Rector pulled a chair up for her, and she sat down, smiling at the two men.

"You interrupted us, you know," Mr. Browning said.

"Did I? What were you talking about? What do men talk about?" Mrs. Ethelburger said.

Mr. Browning poured her out some sherry. "We were not talking," he said.

The Rector swallowed the last drop in his glass and coughed. "Well, time's getting on. I must be off now. All good things come to an end," he said.

The other two politely begged him to stay on, but he would not stay. They watched him out of sight up the drive.

Then Mr. Browning turned to Mrs. Ethelburger. "Why did you come?" he said.

"Aren't I welcome then?" she asked him. "I just brought the flowers. You loved flowers, you said."

"You were not wanted just then," he answered her. "Look how you sent the Rector off!"

"Oh, him," she said.

Mr. Browning leaned towards her, shaking his head. "You see, you miss such a lot not being interested in people, not bothering about ordinary things such as conversation and neighbours," he said. "You have no feeling for kind old men, and you have no feelings about this peaceful evening. You haven't noticed my beautiful fountain playing, and however long I go on talking like this, it won't mean anything to you. Why have you come here? Do you know, you have only been down here about six or seven times all the time we have known each other. Not counting duty visits, and when you wanted something from me, of course. It's nearly dinnertime. Tell me what you want now; or did you really just come to bring those roses?"

"I felt suddenly awfully lonely," Mrs. Ethelburger said.

"How selfish," Mr. Browning said. He leaned back in his chair and closed his eyes.

"How's John?" he said.

"Very well," she replied.

"And your mother and the children and everything else?"

"All very well."

"And you have suddenly become awfully lonely. Well, well, well! And what are we going to do about that?"

"Don't forget, Lawrence, we have to meet each other next Saturday at the Noyces' dinner-party."

"No, Barbara, I know that. But I don't understand. What exactly is the meaning of this *tête-à-tête*?" Mr. Browning sat up again.

"Oh, well, you like flowers, you like me," said Mrs. Ethelburger. "We don't have to say good-bye."

"And you couldn't wait a week to tell me that?" said Mr. Browning.

Mrs. Ethelburger smiled. "But I was lonely," she said, "and besides, the flowers would have died."

Mr. Browning scattered the roses off the table with his hands.

"Damn your flowers," he said.

Mrs. Ethelburger got up from her chair and, walking over the scattered roses, went off without saying any more.

Old Mrs. Browning beat the gong for supper as soon as she saw her going up the drive.

Mr. Browning faced his fat, wrinkled old mother across the dining-room table. "It's good we don't have to talk at meal-times," he said. "All the same, I've got something I want to say to you, Mother."

"You eat," she said. "It cost me a lot of trouble, your chittlings. Don't you go spoiling things with worrying. I can see there's something on your mind. Let it wait, Son, you can't get the goodness out of chittlings when they're cold. And you'd have to shout, for my ears aren't sharp enough for talk at table."

So they finished the meal in silence, and afterwards Mrs. Browning made a cup of tea and came and sat beside her son. "Now you talk," she said.

"It's very difficult," said Mr. Browning. "You see, Mother, you make me so comfortable. But really, I ought to settle down now. I'm forty-one." He sighed, stirring the sugar lumps round and round in his tea.

"So you're serious, are you? Who is it, Son? Not someone from the village?" Mrs. Browning said.

"No. Not that frivolous woman with the roses, if that's who you mean," he answered. "I'm not a home-breaker. I want to make a home. But I've got such a good one already. You don't make it easy for me, Mother."

"You're taking it hard yourself," she said. "Trouble shared is trouble halved. But a new daughter in the house is something for rejoicing. I'll make her welcome, you don't have to fear about that."

"Oh, any pretty girl would do really, I suppose," Mr. Browning said. "But then, they can be tiresome when they're young. It's all so difficult. Can you think of anyone you'd get on with, for instance?"

"So I'm the one that does the choosing for you, am I?" said Mrs. Browning. Her hand shook a little, and some tea fell on her lap from her cup. Her son got out his handkerchief and gently wiped it away.

"Don't be angry, Mother, don't upset yourself," he said. "I shouldn't have spoken. It's just an idea with me that keeps on turning up. You remember last time how we talked it out, how we went over it, you and me. And it's always I who get upset, moithered you'd say. So don't you start now. I'd never, never leave you. You know that."

"There you go, like your father," Mrs. Browning said. "Puzzle and torment a woman, and then making out it's she to blame. But I'm not the one to stand in your way. It's time you took a wife; you listen to your mother."

Mr. Browning patted her hand and looked down on her affectionately. "Well," he said, "I've said it before, and I'll say it again—you look out for someone nice for me. Now I must do a bit of work."

"Silly boy," she muttered to herself as he was leaving the room.

Mr. Browning went to his study and opened his brief-case. "Ah!" he said. He loved his work.

But a little later on he paused in his writing. The scent of creeper coming through the window reminded him that he had forgotten to turn off the fountain. Stepping out on to the verandah, he saw the flowers lying on the bricks where he had scattered them. They looked black by moon-light. He stooped to pick them up. Some movement behind him made him start violently. It was only his mother.

"What are you doing, grovelling about on your knees?" she said in a cross voice. "You'll catch your death. And you never turned off the fountain. All that water going to waste! I can see it from my window."

"All right, all right, for God's sake!" he said.

She went away grumbling.

In the Ethelburgers' house it was quiet at last. The cats lay asleep on the sofa, and the dogs slept huddled up by the dying fire, sighing every now and then and stretching, not quite at rest. The grandfather clock on the staircase landing struck eleven. Mrs. Flint, Mrs. Ethelburger's mother, who slept on the top floor next to the children's bedrooms, closed her book and set her clock right for the morning. Then she took some sleeping-pills, one more than the doctor had prescribed because she was so afraid of not sleeping, and lay down and turned out the lamp. As the clock finished striking, Mrs. Ethelburger cried out and woke up from her sleep.

"John! John!" she cried.

But she was alone in the big bedroom. She turned on the light.

John Ethelburger was at his desk, doing the accounts. He had just about finished, and was thinking of putting the dogs out and shutting up for the night when he heard the sound of slippers coming down towards his room along the stone-flagged passage. He turned his head and waited. It was his wife. She opened the door and came in.

"I'm coming, I'm coming," he said. "You must let me finish my work. Why aren't you in bed?"

"I had a horrible dream," Mrs. Ethelburger said. "I couldn't stay alone up there any more."

"A dream? A dream?" her husband said. He glanced down at his papers and struck out something with the pen he still held in his hand. "Don't worry. I'll be with you in a moment. You can tell it to me in bed." He turned towards her again and smiled. But she looked as though she might be going to cry, so he said, "Oh, Barbara—just like your own children. Do you remember how you went to them when they cried out in the night, and said to them, 'Go to sleep, go to sleep now, it will be all right in the morning.' Is that what you want me to say to you now?"

But she was not comforted. "I dreamed that they cut out the tongues of pigeons to make them sing," she said. "They trapped the pigeons that should have been free in the wood, and they cut their tongues out to make them sing."

Mr. Ethelburger sighed. "I can't think why you should dream these things," he said. "Who's been cutting out your tongue to make you sing? Am I so cruel to you? What have I done wrong?"

"It's not you," Mrs. Ethelburger said. "It was like this. I was walking down a long, straight road with many children. We were an army and we had banners, and they laughed and sang. But I could not keep in step. I saw that soon we must meet another army which was coming towards us in the distance down the long, straight road, and that there would be a battle; for they too had banners and were singing and marching. I cried out to warn the children, to turn them back, to stop them marching. But they would not listen. And I left them, and I came to a market and stopped by a stall where birds were laid out on a marble slab. I touched them, and they were warm and singing to themselves, and not dead. And as I looked at them I saw their suffering, their pain, for their wings had been clipped and their tongues had been cut out! I picked one of them up and held it between my hands. It was a wood-pigeon. I remembered how they sing to themselves in the larch trees in the morning and the evening, peacefully complaining. Yes. And what harm had they done? What had they done that they should be tortured and maimed like that? Who had done this wicked thing? I looked up and saw the stall-keeper smiling down at me. He had a fat red face that always smiled. 'Don't hold them,' he said; 'you can't stop their suffering. You see, we trap them and cut their wings and tongues so that they shall sing for us. It is so beautiful that singing, and when they are wild they do not sing.' 'But they do! they do!' I said. He spread his hands out and went on smiling. 'Only now and then,' he said, 'and who can hear them?' I put down the pigeon on the marble slab as gently as I could, and turned away. I saw the children coming marching down the road. I ran to join them."

Mr. Ethelburger looked down at his hands in silence for a few moments after his wife had finished speaking. Then he said, "If that's what you consider the world has done to you, it's very difficult for me to speak. But haven't you any sense of responsibility? Don't you see, if nothing's ever your fault, it makes you impossible to live with?"

"I don't ask you to be kind to me," she said, "but I did think you'd understand."

"Understand? Of course I do!" he said. "Now look here, who is it goes out shooting wood-pigeons? Me of course. Didn't you see me go out with my gun? And you know as well as I do, pigeons are not so harmless. They spoil my corn. Do you see?"

"I never thought of that," Mrs. Ethelburger said. "No. Well we seem to have got ourselves in rather a muddle." He stretched out his arms and yawned. "Isn't it awfully late?" he said. "Must we go into the hell you're busy making for yourself just now? Let's leave it till the morning, and go to bed now and dream of something else."

"Yes. But how am I going to forget?" she said. Mr. Ethelburger pulled down the top of his rolltop desk. "Like that!" he said. "Come on now. I've had about enough, don't be silly."

He tucked her arm through his arm, and they walked along into the sitting-room together. The dogs woke up at their approach, and yawned and wagged their tails.

"Come on—out you go!" Mr. Ethelburger called them. "I suppose your mother must have a fire?" he said to his wife. "I must say it does seem rather extravagant these warm days."

"Poor mother, she feels the cold so," Mrs. Ethelburger said.

They put the dogs out and locked the front door, and went up the stairs to bed.

"You're not angry my saying that about your mother?" Mr. Ethelburger said on the landing.

"No. Why should I be?" she said.

"I don't know. You seem so ready to take offence, I thought you might feel slighted," her husband said.

Mrs. Ethelburger opened the door of their bedroom and went on in ahead. "Why must you always think of such trivial things to make a fuss about?" she said. "I don't mind—go on and hate my mother, if you want to. That's what men do, they always hate their wife's mother." She waited while he closed the door behind him. "But what do you think I'd do without mother?" she said then. "Who have I got to help me with the children? Who have I got to help me cook and do the washing? Who helps me. . . . ?"

But perhaps you've had enough of Mrs. Ethelburger. Everyone likes heroes or heroines. "There goes a balanced personality," we say (or whatever it is that constitutes our ideal). But if you look at people at all closely, live or work with them—anything that brings them into your life so that they are no longer strangers—you often find they are not heroes or heroines any more. The world is round, however, and your point of balance may be an uncomfortable position for anyone else. But the fact remains, we like some people and we don't like others. I chose Mrs. Ethelburger as heroine because she had love affairs and that sort of thing: this is a story, and one must stick to the conventions. But reading about these people may prove to be like living or working with them, only I promise to stop if it looks like getting too difficult for you.

Now there is just one more person I would like to introduce before I get on. We have already seen that Mrs. Flint (Mrs. Ethelburger's mother) can't sleep at night. She has something on her conscience, her doctor tells her. She doesn't like being spoken to like that. The sleeping-pills she takes are not dangerous; she gets them in a little round box, six at a time—not a fatal dose, you can trust these doctors. But the pills don't help very much to make her sleep.

She has given up trying to get to sleep now, and is knitting something for her daughter. People say, "Poor Mrs. Flint. She has given up her life for her daughter." This may be true. She still has a husband (but he lives in Australia and so is not in this story), and the only one she says she loves is Barbara. And this also may be true. Her face is what village people call "good and kind." Mothers-in-law are taboo in some societies, you may not look at them or speak to them at all; but with us, laughter is permissible, and how we laugh at the dear old mother-in-law situation! It is all a matter of conventions. Either way it's nothing to do with a mother-in-law being good and kind that results in her being treated with such peculiar deference. Just the same, she may be like that. All mothers must give up their lives for a certain amount of time for their children; it is taken for granted that this should be so. But there are objections when mothers go on giving themselves up too long: "They won't let go," it is said. Perhaps there is logic in it.

"How sharper than a serpent's tooth it is to have a thankless child!" Mr. Flint writes from Australia. (But that is another story. He is talking about all the money spent on Barbara's education, and look how she won't even lend him a penny now. And so on.)

Here we are in the Ethelburger household. It is Sunday after lunch. The children are out on the farm with their father, and Mrs. Flint is sewing by the drawing-room window. Mrs. Ethelburger lies on the sofa with two cats purring on her lap. Mrs. Flint has just broken the silence.

"Barbara," she said, "don't you think you might buy a few comfortable chairs? I'm sure John wouldn't mind, if you asked him."

"Um," Mrs. Ethelburger said.

"No, Barbara, do try. You could make this room look so nice if you took a little trouble with it."

"What's the matter? I gave it a good turn out only yesterday."

"No, it isn't that I mean," Mrs. Flint said. "How can I explain it—I mean, perhaps John doesn't notice things; the leather coming off that sofa, for instance, and the chairs being scratched. And look how bare this room is—only those little hunting prints on the wall—no real pictures and not even a vase of flowers anywhere. And Barbara, you used to be so fond of flowers. What do you say to us two making a start, say to-morrow, trying to make the place a little more homely?"

"It's no good trying to change things. This is John's house," Mrs. Ethelburger said.

"Oh, but dear, yours too, you live in it."

"Yes. With all my worldly goods I thee endow," Mrs. Ethelburger said. "Generous. But I've given him four children, haven't I? Or must I go on and on saying thank you?"

"I quite understand how you must feel sometimes," Mrs. Flint said. "But I hope you don't speak like that to John. It's no good rubbing a man up the wrong way. Like that, you make them sensitive. After all, he does a great deal for you, dear. Look how he takes the children off your hands, for instance. It's not every man who would do that."

Mrs. Ethelburger sat up.

"Then they ought to, Mother!" she said. "Good Lord, I had all the bother with them when they were little. Do you think I *liked* all that washing and scrubbing and filthy napkins? Do you think it was fun when they kept me up all night? Honestly, Mother, one can't go on doing one's duty for ever. I liked carrying them. Yes, and I liked feeding them. I did all that perfectly happily and naturally. But look at these cats—they don't go on fussing and mewing round their children for ever. Do they?"

"Human beings are not cats. It is a problem," said her mother.

"And you know I never liked children really," Mrs. Ethelburger said.

"Perhaps you should never have had any?"

"John wanted them. And besides, that's what women are made for."

"We are not machines," Mrs. Flint said severely.

"No, but it's a man's world, and we can't change it," Mrs. Ethelburger said. She lay down again on the sofa.

There was a long silence. Mrs. Flint finished the hem of the sheet she was sewing. Then she said: "I'm not clever, and I'm not adventurous; you get that from your father. I accept things; they are how they are. But I don't kick against the pricks. That is my way, and perhaps it hasn't brought me any great happiness. But it does seem to me, darling child, that unless you put your heart and soul into it, give yourself to it in some way, life isn't going to bring you the least happiness. Not even the small comforts that women lean upon, like having a home, healthy children, and, above all, a good husband. And if you don't value these things, what do you want? What are you looking for? Forgive me, darling, but when I lie awake at night I think and wonder so much about you. Because it isn't too late for you to change if you want to change. You don't have to accept, like I do. Each to his own salvation—I feel very strongly about people being themselves."

"Yes," said Mrs. Ethelburger, "and who am I? The mother of four children."

"And they do mean something to you?"

"Well, there they are," said Mrs. Ethelburger, pointing at the window. "I must get their tea."

Mrs. Flint jumped up from her chair. "No, no, you stay where you are," she said, "I can do that for you."

Mrs. Ethelburger sighed and leaned back again on the cushions.

By now Mr. Blonsom has had time to spread his little piece of gossip about the goings-on up at the Manor. It is often a refreshment to dwell on other people's sufferings, and Mrs. White, who scrubs the floors and washes up and does all the hard work at the Rectory besides keeping her own home spotless and caring for her family, Mrs. White is very interested in suffering. She has rheumatism in the winter and eczema in the summer, and her husband is deaf. She is religious and likes to think about the Day of Judgment. Just now she is pouring out cups of tea from a large, shiny brown teapot for her two girls Pat and Dorothy, while Mr. White taps away at the shoes he is mending in a shed just outside the kitchen window.

"It's sad how some people spend their lives," Mrs. White said.

"Oh, Mum, give it a rest. Pat and me don't often get the chance to go out of an evening. Besides, it was Saturday night!" her daughter said.

Mrs. White sniffed. "I wasn't talking about that," she said.

"What's on your mind, then, Mum?" asked Pat.

"It's the awful things you hear about them at the Manor," Mrs. White said.

The two girls lifted their heads and stared up at their mother with innocent clear eyes, whilst she told them about Mrs. Noyce's defects.

It was good to have something nasty to say about Mrs. Noyce. She had once made the mistake of painting Mrs. Wymondly's portrait. Mrs. Wymondly up at the farm was related to most people in the village (they were a closely related bunch) and Mrs. Noyce hadn't painted a flattering portrait—nobody had a neck like that, and she'd given the poor woman shadows under the eyes as though she'd been drinking. Mrs. White, sister to Mrs. Wymondly, got her own back.

"'Tisn't as though she ever did a stroke of work or ever had to care for her own," she told the girls, "and it's a sad thing for a man to have nobody to follow after him. I daresay Mr. Noyce takes it real hard sometimes. He doesn't look a happy man. If she took an interest in the garden like the old lady used to, that would be better than nothing. But, as your uncle used to say when he worked up there, 'I'd rather have the Old 'Un poking her nose into my seed-boxes than this one snipping at the flowers behind my back.' And now there's nobody to really care for the garden. It's the same inside as out. She doesn't even go round with a duster. Just sits about all day painting. They say she's got enough pictures now to cover all the walls with, and that's a very big place up there. Funny sort of life for a woman. I shouldn't be surprised if there was something queer in her family. But it'll all come out one day."

A hard-working woman who feels herself exploited is somewhat relieved of her burdens when she can express herself this way. And yet, coming from church that morning, Mrs. White had fairly glowed with love for her neighbours. Walking home rather fast to be on time with the Sunday dinner, she was thinking all the while about the sermon. "Love one another," Mr. Spark had said, his deep voice trembling a little. "Love one another." He rarely spoke for more than ten minutes on a Sunday morning, aware that for most of his congregation dinner was the important thing about Sunday. He was fond of them all, and in spite of every evidence to the contrary, believed in the essential goodness of humanity. And that morning he had opened his heart. More than one had gone away uplifted and refreshed. But emotional people (and they are the ones who can be played upon and led) are unstable creatures.

"Love and hate are two sides of the same thing," John Ethelburger had said on his way home. He was, of course, a thoroughly well-educated man, and such an idea would not have occurred to Mrs. White, for instance. Mr. Ethelburger liked complications. Living the simple life, some people call it, when a man buries himself in the country and works his own farm; but people who talk like that can have no idea what it means to own a combine harvester, nor the calculations that have to be made if one wants to breed pedigree cattle successfully, and fatten pigs for ham, and so on and so on. And, of course, at the same time bring up one's own family. This last had proved far and away the most difficult thing, though not necessarily the most complicated.

"It would all be so easy if only you took my advice and followed some sort of a plan," John Ethelburger was often heard saying.

CHAPTER THREE

HALF circled by a wood of larch trees and on the south side open to the sun, there was a lake on Mr. Noyce's property; and on the lake there lived a swan. When she was young and they were young, nurse used to bring her charges here to play on summer afternoons. There were three of them: Lettice, Marianne and little Harry (Mr. Noyce). After they had played and shouted for a time and were in danger of becoming quarrelsome and boisterous, nurse used to tell them stories. If they had been good children and hadn't paddled too far in so as to get their clothes wet, she told them the story of the Seven Swans. This was about a little Princess who had to make seven jackets out of nettles in order to change her brothers back again from swans. She managed it, nurse said, all but one, and there was the seventh brother still swimming on the lake in the likeness of a swan. The children enjoyed that story; it had just the right amount of local colour tinged with day-dream to make it seem happening like their own lives. There was another sort of story for naughty children. "Punishment," nurse called it simply. Whatever rules had been disobeyed or whatever had occurred that day to call down her wrath on little children's heads, nurse spoke of as "wickedness," and inevitably those who had been wicked were carried to the bottom of the lake to be chained beneath the waters for ever and for ever by roots and underhanging branches and underwater weeds. This story quite often caused tears, but whether or not it made the children unhappy it would have been impossible to judge; they were impressed and harrowed. Both stories were the sort that live on in imaginative minds, so that in a manner of speaking this place was enchanted. Lettice, in reality now a decayed gentlewoman living in a service flat in Putney, would return in imagination to the borders of the lake. And Marianne, who had done well for herself and married a rich husband, remembered too, and tried to feel a way back there from servant problems, crises on the Stock Exchange and all the things rich people feel so bitterly. Mr. Noyce had quarrelled badly with his sisters after the death of their father. For one thing, they had both wanted the old nurse to come and work for them in their homes, but Mr. Noyce had indignantly refused to consider it. And there were other more bitter differences about money matters connected with the will. So there were no family gatherings at the Manor, and Mr. Noyce alone of the three children was privileged to continue his days by the side of the lake, should he choose to do so.

There, then, in that idyllic spot Mr. Noyce lies full length in the sun. He is worrying about money. It goes so fast. Once, as a young man, he had considered making some. But his education had not fitted him to the task, and what with the warnings of his mother on the subject of his delicacy (he had once had fits), and the rather brutal letters from his father concerning his career at Oxford, which had not been brilliant, Mr. Noyce had chosen to lead a quiet and moderately scholarly life, abroad for the most part, where his allowance went farther. Then his parents had both died within a week of each other—at a most difficult time because income-tax was going up and up and death duties were enormous. But still, he had inherited a tidy sum. He married and came to live on his estate, and on and off ever since he had started to worry in earnest about making money.

But suddenly he hears footsteps. He opens his eyes, and there through the wood comes Barbara Ethelburger. He waits till she is close enough to be really startled.

"I suppose you know you're trespassing?" he says.

Mrs. Ethelburger nearly jumped into the lake.

Mr. Noyce sat up.

"Oh dear! It's you!" she said. "I thought it was your father."

"Do you often commune with the dead?" he asked.

"Don't be silly. Oh, you did give me such a fright," she said. "I often used to come here. Your father never minded. I hope I didn't disturb you, though. It's such a lovely place here."

"Is it?" said Mr. Noyce. "Well, it's damned expensive."

Mrs. Ethelburger looked down on him with no particular expression on her face.

"Aren't you going to go away?" he said. But instead of provoking her, he was himself provoked by her reply.

"Yes, of course," she said, "but just one minute—I've got that odd feeling that all this has happened before. You know what I mean?"

Mr. Noyce got up and began dusting himself. "Oh yes," he said, "that has all been accounted for—it's very easily explained, you know. Nothing mysterious about that, I assure you. Something about brain-fag or lag—a chemical thing. Oh really, it's a bore. It's not a bit interesting."

His voice got loud, and he gesticulated during this explanation.

"So it's all a matter of glands and pipes and things, is it?" asked Mrs. Ethelburger in a dreamy voice.

"Oh, really! Really!" Mr. Noyce said.

She took no notice, but went on, "One might just as well throw oneself in the lake, then."

"Why not? Why not?" Mr. Noyce cried out.

She looked at him. "Well, why not?" she said.

"Because it's horrid getting wet," Mr. Noyce replied, going over to the edge of the lake and peering down into its depths. A thought had struck him.

"You know old nurse?" he said. "Of course you know her, because you knew my father—well, when we were little children—" He paused a moment.

"Look here," he said, "let's get away from this place. Come indoors. Come and have tea."

After the awkwardness of spreading jam on bread and butter with large knives and with small plates balanced on the knee (sandwiches were beyond Linda, as were different sorts of cutlery), conversation began to flow. Mrs. Noyce was glad to have a visitor that day, she put herself out to charm. Her guest responded with an animation which brought Mr. Noyce out of his internal broodings.

A clock on the mantelpiece struck five, gently; but pleased with themselves and each other, no one paid any attention.

"When first I came here," Mr. Noyce was saying, "I thought I should die of boredom. Of course I lived here as a child, but I'd got used to seeing people and travel and town life. But now I like the way things change here—so reasonably and slowly, and I'm glad to be rid of the noise and the hurry."

"I suppose I'd paint wherever I was," his wife said. "The trouble is, Harry and I are both so unsociable."

"But you like people," said Mrs. Ethelburger. "You don't prefer dogs to men, for instance."

"We like acquaintances, not friends. I think that's it," Mr. Noyce said. "I've got some friends, of course, scattered about the place. But they're nice, quiet people like ourselves who don't go in for tragedies. That's the trouble with village life, anything unpleasant that happens is felt all over the place. One only has to look at Mrs. Spark to be reminded that her son is dead. And all those tombstones with familiar names! What friendships one would have to strike up with the dead if one wanted to make friends with the living! I'm not unsympathetic towards all this giving birth to and marrying and dying; but you know, if one pays too much attention to that sort of thing one never gets *on* with it, never gets on with the process—to make use of one's time, to do whatever it is one's experience inclines one towards—to live. And I can't make friends with people who don't feel the same about it."

"What a pity one can't have everything. One is always giving up," his wife said.

"But you know," Mr. Noyce went on, "women very seldom have the feeling that they have their own lives to lead. It's always their children or their husbands or their houses. And it doesn't make them any happier, I notice, living for others."

"But nobody really lives for other people," Mrs. Ethelburger said. "It's just the way things happen. It's so difficult to strike out and make a way for one's self; you have to be an uncomfortable person to do that. Or there is the missionary spirit. There's no missionary spirit in me. I don't see how you could possibly make people better or worse; they change if there's room in themselves for change, and then blame each other for what goes on. Of course, as my husband says, one should have a sense of responsibility. But it doesn't come naturally. I mean, it has to be learned like Shakespeare and Eng. Lit., and how to behave at table and so on. You know, I can't help thinking about your father. He was old and wise, and I trusted what he said. And besides, he listened to me. To get away from the children a bit, I used to come to the lake, your lake, a quiet place where one can remember things in peace. Sometimes I met him there, and once I told him about my childhood, my happiest days. But he said, no, children lead violent lives—I had forgotten the unhappiness; and yet it was the past that made one beautiful. So this afternoon I came to the lake again. And for some reason, as I walked through the wood, I thought of the Rector's son. You said you don't like tragedies, but calling what happens a tragedy is what you feel about it—just a label, because things are not cruel or kind in themselves, they are just what happened. Well, he was dead when I saw him in the river, floating and turning slowly round and round. They had just got the boat out. We waited. It didn't seem real, but I knew that it was. There must have been something sudden and desperate once, but all that was done, and the river flowed on, first with him, and then without him." She stopped.

"Oh, I think it's terrible," Mrs. Noyce said. "Just think, it was their only child. Fate or God or whatever you call it, it's a senseless, wicked thing to happen."

"No, no," Mrs. Ethelburger went on. "He fell in, they found his footsteps on the bank near where the water-lilies grow, he fell in and was drowned. It just happened like everything else. But in such a world how *can* one live happily?"

"But nobody does, my dear," Mr. Noyce said. He let the cigarette smoke out of his mouth slowly. "If you have such passionate feelings," he said, "you ought to be an artist, like Eileen."

"Oughtn't you to be an artist, then?" Mrs. Ethelburger said, turning towards him.

He shrugged his shoulders. "You know, I really don't feel passionate about anything," he said.

"But you talked about getting on with it—living. What did you mean?"

"Oh, just trying to understand and not just being it all."

"Then you think there's a solution, some sort of an answer?"

Mr. Noyce laughed.

"How like a woman!" he said.

"That means he doesn't know, and if he did he wouldn't tell," Mrs. Noyce said.

"Well, it's probably a mistake to bother about such things," Mrs. Ethelburger said. "It makes one boring and nasty. Whenever I get like this at home, there's trouble. I do so hate men when they start being reasonable, because there's one reason for them and another for us. There isn't just one enormous reason for everyone."

"So you like chaos," Mr. Noyce said. The cat came in at the window just then, and settled itself down on his lap. He stroked it and it purred.

"And you like cats," said Mrs. Ethelburger.

"I wouldn't say that," he said. "It's not mine, you know, it's Nurse's." The clock struck the half-hour, and this time they all turned towards it as though summoned.

"I must go," said Mrs. Ethelburger. "I must put the children to bed."

Good material for a diary this conversation, one would have thought; something to note down even if one didn't try to remember every word of it. But late that night Mr. Noyce sat at the table in his study, mute and unhappy. An opened letter from his publishers lies on the floor, where it has fallen from between his fingers.

"DEAR MR. NOYCE (it reads),

"Thank you for sending us the two MSS. 'More Stories for the Children' is excellent, and we would like to get this on the market as soon as possible to be in time for Christmas.

"About 'Change but not Decay.' This is really a collection of philosophical essays, isn't it? And while of course we do publish 'serious works,' as you call them in your letter, philosophy has never been at all popular with our public.

"Perhaps you would like us to return the MS. of 'Change but not Decay'? Or would you rather we kept it here for you until you pay a visit to London? We shall certainly be wanting to see you about 'More Stories for the Children' some time very soon. Meanwhile . . ."

But Mr. Noyce kicks the letter away from him. "Damn them," he says, "half a loaf. . . . And it's not even my bread really."

*

Nurse always stayed up late. She needed little sleep at her age and preferred to doze before the fire rather than lie in darkness in her bed. Her eyes were too tired to read after supper. She often sat rocking herself backwards and forwards with the Bible on her knees, staring at the fire, the cat in front of her, inside the fender. She was rocking herself like this, backwards and forwards, when Mr. Noyce came in at eleven o'clock. He closed the door and came over and stood beside her, leaning on the mantelpiece.

"Well," he said, "we're going to get those stories published."

"I saw you had a letter after tea. I'm so glad, Master Harry," she said. There was a silence. "Aren't you pleased, then?" she asked him.

"It's you who should be pleased. My work hasn't been accepted," he said.

Nurse clicked her tongue. "Of course, it's all your work now! Who writes it all down? Who has all the trouble with it?" she asked. "Any old woman, you know as well as I do, has a lot of rubbish in her head. But it isn't everyone can make it sense and write it down. You make it sound so lovely. It's because you don't put your own name to it, you feel it's not your own. I'd be proud to see 'Henry Noyce' outside a book, if I were you. It's such a literary name."

"So would I," said Mr. Noyce, "on *my* book."

"Well, it's no use arguing with you," nurse said, "but if you'd read it out to me, just a bit of it, perhaps I could help you with *your* book."

"It's not the sort of thing you'd ever read, Nurse," he said. "It's too difficult, too—well, how shall I say—too . . ."

"Much too difficult, Master Harry. Just like yourself. You always did take the hard way."

"I don't. I take things easy."

Nurse sighed. "Your father used to call you lazy," she said, "but you're not lazy. You think too long about a thing and get into a muddle. You can't be simple. That's your trouble. I expect your book's like that. You want to make it simple; then they'd have it. I know they would."

But Mr. Noyce paid no attention. He was thinking of something else. "Chained to the bottom of the lake—do you remember that one, Nurse? We might have that in our next one. And that doesn't need any acknowledgments. It's your own, isn't it? What was it called? I know—'Punishment.' Odd, you know, I thought of it this afternoon, but it went out of my head. And then I dare say we could think up six or seven more between us, couldn't we? They don't want big books, because the little horrors like them small and handy. That's what we'll do. So off you go to bed, Nurse, and think up 'Punishment.'"

"I shall do nothing of the sort," nurse said. "Fancy giving little children names like that! And I'd never tell them such a story. That was meant for a purpose, it wasn't meant to please."

"Does one always have to please? Oh well, I'm sorry," Mr. Noyce said. "Let's forget about it now. I'm upset about my book, that's what it is. You know what I am."

"You ought to talk things over with Miss Eileen a bit more, you know," nurse said.

Mr. Noyce frowned.

"Miss Eileen is an artist," he said after a pause. "I mean that quite seriously. One day she will paint, and her pictures may be remembered. I'm not an artist, not by a long way. So even if she thinks I'm a bit ridiculous with my stories, I'm still going to go on in my own way, because that way I can earn a little money—just a little money. It's a pity the stories are so old-fashioned, otherwise we might try America. They say I wouldn't find a public in America."

"We shall have to see what we can do, then. Perhaps it wouldn't do them any harm to have 'Punishment' over there. And now it's bed-time, Master Harry," nurse said.

CHAPTER FOUR

VERY early in the morning when the sun behind the trees cast long shadows on the lawn, Mr. Browning walked about his garden. Sometimes he got up early like this so that he might have an hour or two by himself before going off in his car to the station and to work. But all through his life he had suffered from attacks of migraine, which started by making him feel restless and depressed. Mr. Browning was a Spartan about illness. He never took pills or medicines, and refused to have injections. He called his attacks of migraine "just nonsense" when he hadn't got one, and when one of them started went on with his work until in a state of collapse. All this caused his mother to worry about him acutely. A nice case for a psycho-analyst! But Mr. Browning knows all about that. In fact, during a convalescent period after the war he amused himself writing short stories (not intended for publication), collectively entitled "Tales told to a Trick Cyclist." He had not enjoyed himself in the army.

He could not have said this morning whether he was going to have one of his attacks. But he talked to himself; a bad sign his mother would have told you. The day is fresh after a night of rain and Mrs. Ethelburger's children are out in the meadows picking mushrooms already. Smoke goes straight up in the air from cottage chimneys. Mrs. Browning is switching on the hot plates in her kitchen for breakfast; her son insisted she should have nothing but the best and most modern. The house is full of gadgets—but Mr. Browning is outside in the garden.

"Nice little person," he says to one of his chrysanthemums, and bends down to have a look at it. It is a dwarf kind and, like many other plants in this garden, rather rare. Then he goes on to the dahlias. "Come on!" he says, "we want a bit of colour." He examines them for earwigs. He sighs and goes on talking to himself. "What a lot of work. Two gardeners! And I'd be worth two myself if only I had the time. Too much to do," he says. He wanders off. We need not follow him among the cabbages in the vegetable garden; but coming out, between the two box hedges, he suddenly turns round and walks back fast along the way he has come. He is not going where the dahlias are, however; he takes the path towards the roses.

"Ridiculous!" he says to the roses, examining their heads. "Quite ridiculous. But what is a man to do? Oh, I'm sick of it, God knows. And I don't have to come here to be reminded—huh! The next thing it'll be, she'll be putting me off my work! But she's not going to put me off my roses." He held a yellow rose between his fingers, and with great care examined its petals. "Now what's the matter with you, Mrs.?" he said. "Looks as though you needed a bit of attention. I'll have to come home early this evening."

It was then that Mrs. Browning called out: "Lawrence! Lawrence—wherever are you? Breakfast's ready!" And he put his hands up over his head. The migraine had started.

His mother watched him during breakfast. She knew he was in pain; his colour had gone and he never stopped blinking. "Come home early, if you can," she said to him afterwards in the hall.

He snatched the car keys which she had found for him.

"Impossible," he said. "Don't ask me what time I'll be back—you'll have to expect me when you see me."

Instead of getting on with the housework after he had gone, Mrs. Browning went straight away to her son's room where he worked. He kept the door locked (he insisted on this privacy), but in finding the key of the car she had also found the key that unlocked this door. She stood and listened a moment before sitting at the table. But there were only ordinary sounds. She took out her spectacles and sat down. The table was covered with papers. She looked at them, and then picked them up and had a look underneath. Then she opened the table drawers and very carefully looked through the papers there. "Nothing but work," she muttered to herself, "but he must keep them somewhere. Or doesn't he keep them?" She went all through the papers again. But what she wanted wasn't there. After about half an hour, she gave up searching and picked up the typewriter to put it in its place in front of her where it had been when she came in. There was a sheet of ordinary quarto paper stuck in the typewriter with two words typed out on it. She hadn't noticed this before, but now she looked.

"Dear Barbara," she read. There was nothing more.

"So *he* writes to *her*," Mrs. Browning said.

She got up and leaned on the table with her knuckles.

"That's bad," she said. "Now what are we going to do about it. Oh, I wish I'd never come in here. But it was *her* letters I was after. This isn't like my boy, not my son." She took off her spectacles and wept.

Old people weep easily; like very young children, they need someone to comfort them, otherwise they go on sobbing. But Mrs. Browning had never pitied herself for long. She was a courageous old lady (and it had needed a good deal of courage to play the spy on her son), and after about five or ten minutes she was able to pull herself together. But in her distress she left her spectacles behind on the table when she went.

As for Mr. Browning, he nearly had an accident on his way to the station. He was driving very fast and met a cyclist coming round a corner on the wrong side of the road. It was a near thing. The shock of this made him more careful. Arriving at the station, he found he had a quarter of an hour to wait before his train was due. He walked up and down the platform, muttering to himself, and then all at once went into the waiting-room reserved for First Class passengers. Here he opened his despatch-case, and, taking out an Eversharp pencil and some sheets of paper, began to write furiously, with an angry expression on his face. He only stopped writing after the train was signalled. Then he bought a packet of envelopes at the stationer's on the platform, borrowed a stamp from the ticket collector (a man who knew him well), and ran across the bridge over the line to post the letter just as his train came in. He nearly missed that train. The letter was in time for the 9 A.M. collection, and so was delivered at the farm by half-past five that evening.

Mrs. Ethelburger looked at it, surprised. She didn't recognise the writing. She was just going to have a look at the bees before putting the children to bed. She had on a wide-brimmed hat with a black veil over it, and wore a pair of her husband's old trousers with socks tucked over the bottoms, and black gloves tucked in at the wrists. Her hand was on the door handle to open it when the letter fell through the letter-box. She took off a glove now to open the letter. The black veil made it difficult to read. She turned the pages over to find the signature. The children came running down the stone passage round the corner. She stuffed the letter into a pocket and went out to do the bees.

The bees needed a great deal of attention, and for the next hour or so Mrs. Ethelburger was hard at it, taking in the honey. They were her bees, but she was not yet expert, and got stung. The younger children were already in their bath when she came in. She took off her rather peculiar clothes, and left them on the bedroom floor before going into the bathroom. Now her mother, Mrs. Flint, was one of those people who will tidy up after others; she had noticed her daughter's face swelling up where she was stung, and she wanted to help. So she went into Mrs. Ethelburger's bedroom to tidy it up. The trousers on the floor and the hat were the first things that caught her eye. She picked the trousers up by the legs and shook them. The letter fell out of the pocket. Mrs. Flint was not in the habit of reading other people's letters—no normal person is—but perhaps because this particular letter was written in pencil she took a little more notice of it than was wise. Most women are curious. And before she knew what she was doing she had read a whole page. Then she heard Mr. Ethelburger coming, so she stuffed it in her pocket and rushed off to her own room. There she read all of that letter. She sat some time with it on her lap after she had finished, staring out of the window.

"Oh, Barbara," she said, "my poor Barbara! We must all be brave." But she had to get the letter back again where she had found it. Only after she had managed to do this did she begin to feel guilty. Meeting her son-in-law in the passage, she excused herself from supper, saying she didn't feel at all well and was going to bed. By this time Mrs. Ethelburger's face had swollen up so that she could only see out of one eye, so with one eye she read the letter.

"Dear Barbara (it said),

"I've wasted about twenty sheets already and I'm not going to try any more, so this will have to do. Two days ago I was engaged to be married, who to doesn't matter, you don't know her. I was going to keep it a surprise till the dinner party. I wanted to hurt you. Forgive me about that. I'm in a hurry, so I can't try to explain things and there isn't time for me to be dignified or clever as I'd like to be, and of course I never write this sort of letter. I tore up all your letters. I had kept them mainly because I felt I had got something against you there. An ugly thing to do. But then I still think, in spite of what you say, that our 'affair,' that's what other people would call it, is essentially ugly. I don't think you like people being really fond of you, otherwise you wouldn't behave as you do. And I don't believe you are as mean and petty-minded as you try to make out you are. What possible pleasure can it give you to keep me dangling on a string? I watched you very carefully when you brought those roses—I believe it hurt you to behave like that. Well, I have told no one—not even my mother—about my engagement, except you, which was lucky, because yesterday I broke the whole thing off. I thought it was going to make me free, and I could patch up things again with my mother and live in peace. You see, lately I've been quarrelling with Mother. I felt guilty about getting married and leaving her in the lurch, because it was so obvious I could not get married and go on living with her. But I think she suspected my conduct in relation to you. Women seem to have a nose for 'affairs.' But I am not free. What are you going to do? I cannot meet you at this dinner party without knowing first how I stand. Are we going to meet in London as we used to, or are we to meet only in public and at length to become strangers? You must decide. You know, as well as I do, I shall never get married. Whatever you do, burn this letter as soon as you have read it—you must do this. I have been most indiscreet in writing to you. And make haste and write to me. Only, for heaven's sake, use a typewriter to address the letter, and do not, whatever you do, write to the office.

"In haste,

"Yours,

"L."

"Why should I write to his office? I never have done. He must have been engaged to his secretary," Mrs. Ethelburger said aloud. She touched her swollen face where it was painful, and winced.

"Your mother isn't well," her husband said, coming into the room. "You'd better go and find out what's the matter. She's gone to bed."

"Oh dear. It never rains but it pours," said Mrs. Ethelburger.

"Cheer up," he said, "you're not the first to get stung, and not the last either."

"If it were only that," she said under her breath, but he heard. She thought he might.

"Anything the matter?" he asked.

Mrs. Ethelburger threw the letter in the fire.

"Who writes to you in pencil?"

"Oh, just one of my bloody-minded lovers," she said.

Mr. Ethelburger turned on the wireless. "Well, it's a pity he can't see you, then. You really are a sight," he said. Dance music filled the room. He turned the volume down as she went out.

"My darling! My poor darling!" Mrs. Flint said as her daughter came in. She was in bed. Used to her mother, Mrs. Ethelburger felt, nevertheless, this was an exaggeration of her suffering. She patted her swollen face. "Oh, it's not as bad as all that," she said.

With subdued emotion Mrs. Flint explained about the letter. There was a long pause, and then Mrs. Ethelburger said, "It's a pity. You shouldn't read other people's letters."

It was not long, though, before the two women were in each other's arms, comforted and happy.

"I've known for some time now things weren't right," Mrs. Flint was saying, "but now everything is going to be all right again, isn't it, darling? It's your father's blood in you. You can't help it, it's your father."

"I never wanted to be like him," Mrs. Ethelburger said, "but I did love grandfather. Do you remember when I was little, mother, and we lived with him? And how I loved that house! I still remember every room. And the garden and the yellow jasmin. How happy I was then!"

"Yes, dear child," her mother said; "yes, dear child."

"Old Mr. Noyce could understand—his house reminded me, it was so much the same. Why do I always like old people, Mother? Old people and old places. You must never think I really loved this man," Mrs. Ethelburger said.

"Who was it, dear? Tell me, and then we can forget."

"Oh, then you don't know!" Mrs. Ethelburger leaned back away from her mother. "Well," she said, "I don't think it would be fair to John to tell you. Let's just forget."

"That's a good girl," said her mother.

"I say!" Mr. Ethelburger called out down the passage. "What about supper? Shall I make it?"

The two women looked at each other and smiled, and nodded their heads.

"Run along now and make him a nice omelette. He'll be pleased," Mrs. Flint said.

After all, Mr. Browning did come home early that night. He put the car away and went off at once to see to the roses. He didn't talk much during supper, but his mother was happy because he looked less strained. She herself had rested most of the afternoon, and then just pottered about the place before getting the meal ready. He went into his room immediately after supper and found her glasses on the table. He brought them into the kitchen where she was washing-up (generally he helped), and said, "What have you been doing in my room, Mother?"

The poor old woman bowed her head over the sink. "I shouldn't have done it. I know I shouldn't," she said.

Mr. Browning dropped the spectacles on a chair and clutched his head. It seemed as though he couldn't speak, but when she turned towards him his mother saw his lips moving.

"Don't blaspheme, my son," she said.

"I'm going," Mr. Browning said in a weak voice.

"I'm going. There's no peace anywhere. There's no peace."

His mother filled a kettle full of water and put it on the stove. "Sit down," she said; "then you'll feel better. Mind now, not on my glasses. Now tell us what it's all about. It's no good, you can't keep things from your mother." She put her hands on her hips with her elbows out and waited.

"So it seems," he said. "Oh, my head! Oh, my poor head."

"Never mind about your head now. Let's have it out," Mrs. Browning said.

He told her while the kettle boiled, omitting names. Afterwards they drank their cups of tea in silence, not looking at each other. When he had finished, Mr. Browning got up and said, "Well, now, you've brought it on yourself. You realise we can't possibly go on living together after this, Mother?"

"Oh-ho!" she said. "Listen to him! And where does he think he's going to live? With his airy fairy lady, I suppose. But she's not going to have him. Not she!"

"I shall go and live somewhere quite alone," Mr. Browning said with dignity.

"You try! You just try!" his mother said.

Mr. Browning looked at his watch. It was a new one, the sort that looks rather like a bracelet. "It's getting late," he said. "Don't let's waste time shouting at each other. I've got work to do."

"I'm sure I didn't mean to shout," she said, "but a woman's got to speak her mind sometime." She picked up the cups and saucers and took them over to the sink. "A man's got to have a life of his own, we all know that," she said. "There's man's work and there's woman's work. But there's no sense in all this carrying on. You ought to have a wife, I've always said so, and raise a family like others do. But when a woman feels there's something queer going on behind her back all the time, well then, any decent woman's going to find out what it is. Besides, I am your mother."

The telephone rang.

They looked at each other.

"Go on, answer it!" she said.

"It's not for me. Nobody rings me at home about work," he said, "it's one of your friends."

"Friends?" she said. "Who do you think I've got for friends in this rotten old village? I'm not going to answer the telephone for you every time it rings. What do you think I am?" She turned her back on him. "You're all right," she said. "You can go in the hall and shut the door—I shan't hear what you're saying. I'm not the sort that goes in for listening."

"I know exactly what you're thinking, Mother," Mr. Browning said (controlling himself), "probably it's a wrong number, but I'm going to answer it, just in case."

It stopped ringing as he began to go, so he went off into his study instead.

After Mrs. Browning had finished in the kitchen and had made everything look tidy and usual so that there was nothing unpleasant left over for the next day, she went upstairs to her bedroom and got out the family snapshot album. This was a large, heavy, leather-bound volume given to her by her son with his first earnings, into which she had stuck all the photos, snaps and shiny postcards commemorating family holidays that she possessed. She looked at the old-fashioned ones first, going over the pages slowly, saying, "That's Florence, now, when she was married; that's Uncle Herbert," and so on, as she pointed them out to herself with her finger. "He's dead now," or, "She's gone to live in Birmingham," she would add before going on to the next. All this took a bit of time. She had come to a photo of her husband, and was just shaking her head over him when a door opened downstairs and she heard her son walking across the hall. She was just going over to the window when she heard him coming up the stairs. She ran back to her chair at the table, and was sitting there when he knocked and came into her room.

"Hullo, Mother," he said.

"Hullo, Son. I thought you might be going out to-night," she said.

"Now, that's not fair, Mother. Do I ever go out at night and leave you alone in the house?"

"There's no knowing nowadays."

"Look here, Mother," Mr. Browning said, "I'm not going to be messed about like this any more. It's my life. I've made my mind up. My work is what matters to me. With things all upside down and at sixes and sevens, I can't work properly. I'm a success at my job, and that's what I've always got to be. No woman is going to stop me being what I want to be. Understand?"

"I'm glad, Son, I'm glad," Mrs. Browning said. "I was just coming to the snaps of you taken when you were a little boy. Oh, what a dear little boy you used to be! But you always knew what you wanted, even in those days."

"Did I?" said Mr. Browning. "Well, I am what you call a self-made man, I suppose. Let's have a look at myself in the making."

He sat down at his mother's side, and she moved the album over so that he could see. They turned the pages together. "I wonder what's happened to all those people now," Mr. Browning said, pointing to a group photographed on the sands at Margate. "Well, we've left them behind, haven't we, Mother?"

"Yes, in a manner of speaking," she said. "But it's not all for the good, I wouldn't say. It makes it a bit lonely."

"It's all a matter of will-power really," Mr. Browning said. "Make up your mind and stick to it. That's all it amounts to."

"And choose wisely," his mother said.

"Oh, choice!" said Mr. Browning. "You do what you have to do. I don't see there's any choice in that. Don't you believe it." They turned over a few more pages. "Still," he said, "I must say that I've always hoped that what I *had* to do would be something extraordinary. I mean, if I did find the right woman, you know, Mother, and it was either her or my career, I'd choose her any day. That's what I want—to *have* to choose her—then she'd be worth having. But they're all so ordinary and dull! They want just the ordinary thing—nothing extravagant or wild. Expensive presents—yes—that sort of woman considers herself a valuable toy. And the other sort won't take anything, and the debt you owe her goes on piling up inside her head. Being a businessman makes one very sensitive to things like that. No, they're all just adventuresses without adventure. You wouldn't travel far if you travelled with them."

"You're turning the pages and you're not looking," Mrs. Browning said.

He drew the album towards the light and looked closely at the photographs. "Good people, but rather dull," he said.

"But washing and cooking and scrubbing is dull," his mother said; "dull, and cruel when it's a matter of trying to make ends meet. Now, I remember how your father . . ."

"Don't," said Mr. Browning, interrupting her.

"And why not?" she said. "Aren't you proud . . ."

"It's senseless being proud, it makes you as silly as the rest of them," he said. "Put away your old book, Mother, and come to the party on Saturday. Get to know them— have a chat with Mrs. Noyce and Mrs. Ethelburger and the rest. They're not a bad lot, really."

"What, that woman?" said his mother, "not me. I've nothing to say to her that she'd like to hear!"

"That's unjust," Mr. Browning said, "because you've never even tried to know her. Anyway, I won't go without you."

"Then we don't go," Mrs. Browning said.

Love affairs have their complications. They certainly do.

But in case you think this is all rather half-hearted and not very romantic, I must tell you about Mrs. Broom. To-night she is going to elope with an old friend of hers, one of the circus hands who helps with the tents. Ever since the circus came to the town again, these two have been meeting secretly, and now that the circus is moving on next day, they have decided that they love one another and cannot be parted. It is the right sort of night for romance. The moon is high up in the sky, and all about her moving clouds obscure the brilliance of the stars. There is no wind and the earth smells warm. Mr. Broom is just going out with his gun. Among other things, he is a poacher. Mrs. Broom sits indoors by the window, waiting. The oil-lamp roars and smells on the table where she leans her arms, and the untroubled cats sleep on the hearth-rug by the fire. Time passes. What does Mrs. Broom think about, waiting for her lover? Her face is calm. She fingers the long scar down her cheek where the lion struck her. Isn't she going to do her hair or change her working dress or put some things together in a bag to take with her? Her husband is gone now, over half an hour, perhaps she will never see him again. Does she feel no regret, then, or are her thoughts full of malice towards him? Surely she will at least leave a note for him beside the lamp, so that he will find it when he comes home. But she is calm. Suddenly there are footsteps. She turns her head towards the door and waits. A man comes in without knocking. "Ready?" he says. She goes across the room and takes her coat off the peg at the back of the door.

"I'm ready," she says.

"Told him?" he asks, standing by the doorway.

"What have I got to say?" she says. "I'm just going back home, that's all. We'll have moved on by the time he thinks about the circus. He's not going to bother me any more."

He puts his arm round her waist, and she leads him away.

The cats stare into an emptiness. It has all happened. Seven years, and what will she remember about them? She has taken nothing away with her, just as she brought nothing. The cats will forget their tricks; the little comedy has ended.

There is something sad about this; one of my characters has gone away. I have said very little about Mrs. Broom, and yet her life could have been a whole story, only not my kind of story. Sometimes people do this. They fly in and out of one's life, leaving a brief impression of a world unexplored; their world, which without them one would never have noticed. And yet if they had remained long enough not to have been strangers, they would have fitted in to all one's ideas, so that it is only in their strangeness they would seem to have any importance.

It is Mrs. Ethelburger, of course, who carries on my story. All day long she has been thinking about Mr. Browning's letter, and now the time has come when she must answer it. She goes to the end of the garden, and, sitting down under an old apple tree, begins to write.

"Dear Lawrence," she writes, "thank you for your letter. You were quite wrong. I *was* lonely when I brought those roses to you, and that is why I came. I don't keep people dangling on strings, I go to people when I feel I need their company. And why don't you get married? It is useless trying to put the blame on me.

"If you think of our affair as ugly, let us end it. Only don't try to cold-shoulder me, because however much you may wish it, we can never be real strangers. So when we meet, as we must meet on Saturday, allow me to smile at you when I say good evening, and perhaps we might have a little conversation together before we say good-bye. If you don't do this, who am I going to talk to at the dinner party? You always laugh when I say that you are the only person who doesn't understand me. But talking to you makes me feel, or rather can make me feel, light-hearted. Because I don't have to be on my guard with you—there is no need for me to pretend to be any one at all. Why? Because you take yourself so very seriously, nobody else has any importance. That is how *I* am, other people tell me. When the King of the universe and the Queen of the universe meet, it is of course a very dignified occasion, but also very funny. Don't you feel it's going to be a bit lonely without the Queen—alone with all that Majesty?

"Well, last night I had a dream. You don't have dreams I know, but this one was so vivid I thought, directly I woke, I must tell you. It is dangerous to tell people one's dreams, they might understand, but you don't understand, so there you are, you see. Well, I dreamed that at last after many years I had come home—not to my home, but to my grandfather's house. I had found my way through the maze in the garden and I stood outside looking up at the house. It was night, and the moon shone back at me from the windows of the house and I could not see in. I found the door, and it was not locked. I found myself walking down empty corridors where everything smelled of dust. I thought how easy it had been to enter this house, but how hard it had been to find it. And I went into the drawing-room where we used to have tea with my grandmother. There was nobody there, and there was no furniture and no fire burned in the grate. It was damp, and the dust flew up from the floorboards as I walked and mice ate at the wood. I left this room, and I went upstairs. But wherever I went it was empty and bare. There was no one. And I knew that long ago they had left this house and no one would live there again. So I climbed to the top of the house where I used to sleep as a child. It smelled as it used to smell, of wood shavings and cold water, and the cistern still sighed and dripped. The moon came into my room through the low windows, and there were the stuffed birds inside their glass cages staring with cold glass eyes, and there was my bed. But suddenly I heard voices—people talking, and laughing. I made my way back down the stairs and along the corridors till I came to a room in the very centre of the house, a room where the door stood ajar and from where a golden light shone down the corridor. I listened, and I heard the voices of children talking and laughing. And a young child with a smiling face came out of the room and saw me.

"'Who are you?' I said. And she said, 'But I am always here and the door is never shut.' And I was comforted."

"What are you writing there?" asked Mr. Ethelburger. He looked down on her from the other side of the hedge. "There's such a strange expression on your face. I'm sorry, I didn't mean to startle you."

"Must you always know everything I do? How long have you been watching me—how did you know I was here?" his wife said.

"It's not as difficult as you might think for me to find you, my dear," he said. "I know you always come here when you want to hide yourself, and naturally I wouldn't disturb you unless you were wanted. But when you are wanted and nobody seems to know where you are, this is where I look first. The Rector's wife is in the sitting-room, waiting to speak to you."

"Let me just finish this. It's a letter," Mrs. Ethelburger said. "No more now," she wrote at the bottom of the page, "with love from Barbara."

CHAPTER FIVE

IT IS evening now. The Rector is called in from his garden by a little bell which his wife rings when meals are ready. She has opened the french windows and stands there with her arm raised, ringing and ringing the bell until she hears her husband's voice. "All right, dear," he says.

She drops her arm to her side and goes back into the house, calling over her shoulder, "Do hurry, Arthur—it's kippers, and you know how cold they get."

They have high tea at the Rectory so that Mrs. White can do the washing-up before she goes. This means that Mr. White and the girls are kept waiting for their supper—the same meal as Mrs. Spark's 'high tea,' and the same in essence as the Ethelburger's dinner, only dinner is later and is followed by coffee, not served with tea—but Mrs. White would do anything for the Rector, and she knows the girls will start getting things ready directly they get home, and Mr. White will wait about quite patiently.

"You know, dear, we really must do something about the garden," the Rector said, after he had eaten his kippers. "We've had some lovely flowers this year, thanks to Mr. Browning's help. But I do feel it's up to us to keep the fruit in order. Now, I've bought a book on pruning fruit trees. The pears and apples I shall leave alone, they've grown too big, but I thought if I looked after the raspberries and the little peach tree, you could read about the black currants and do what is necessary. It may not be the right time of year to interfere with them, of course." He sighed.

"If you let the children in to pick up chestnuts, you'll never be able to keep things tidy," Mrs. Spark said.

"Conkers," the Rector said; "oh, they belong to children."

"Yes, but once you let the children in—never mind, though."

"It's hard for you, Clare; I know it is. But don't let's worry about untidiness."

"But they steal," Mrs. Spark said.

"Yes, I know they do. And so do the squirrels. I'm afraid they've rather smashed the little peach tree."

"Oh—and I planted that myself!"

"Well, you won't shoot the squirrels yourself, and I won't shut the children out. It's obvious, we are not gardeners," the Rector said. "All the same," he added, "have a look at the book sometime. I put it in your room. You might be interested."

"Don't forget your tea, Arthur," Mrs. Spark said, "it's getting cold. And when you've finished, there's something I want to tell you."

She began to clear the table, leaving an island of crockery about her husband's place. "There's no need to hurry, though," she said. "I'll just take out what we've finished with, so that Mrs. White can be getting on with it."

The Rector finished his meal in haste. "I'll take my apple in the garden," he said.

The Rectory garden was a large and melancholy place. In bygone days someone had planted willow trees, which now, untended, leaned down in distress over bird-whitened benches. Here and there a bed had been reclaimed from the weedy grass which grew everywhere, so that patches of geranium colour or a bright-red rose disturbed the eye, which might have found tranquillity in a green wilderness. By gentle slopes a path led to the river, and here, in the boathouse, watching the sun sink down, the Rector and his wife had come to talk together.

"It is a lovely evening," the Rector said; "let us enjoy this place and forget our troubles before it gets dark and you complain of the damp."

"Yes, it is peaceful here," she said. "What shall we talk about, Arthur? You know I have something to tell you. But I can put that out of my mind if you would rather discuss the Harvest Festival or something pleasant." She pulled out a bundle of socks from a huge pocket in the middle of her overall and began looking for holes.

"Rest, my dear. Put away your work and sit with your hands folded in your lap," her husband said. "And now tell me what you have to say."

"Well, you must know, Arthur, that Mr. Broom who works for Mr. Noyce has lost his wife," she began. He nodded his head, so she went on, "She ran away."

"I know. I know all that," the Rector said. "There's really no need for you to distress yourself."

"But I'm not in the least distressed, Arthur. Do listen," she said. "Well, about this afternoon. You know we agreed that one or other of us should speak to the Ethelburgers about their little boy who is old enough now to begin instruction for his Confirmation. As I take Sunday-school and therefore know Christopher—quite a nice little boy—I thought it right that I should be the one to broach the subject to his parents. So I went down to the farm to see them. First I talked to Mr. Ethelburger (they couldn't find *her*). Although he is always so jolly and charming, you never quite know with him—know whether he says what he means. So when he said, 'Right you are, you go ahead with Chris,' I said, 'But, you know, I really must have a word with your wife.' Because, after all, Arthur, I like to consult a mother about that sort of thing. He said he would see if he could find her. What an untidy place that is! Dogs have chewed all the carpets, and nothing but hideous leather armchairs. Even so, you get covered with hairs as soon as you sit. But I didn't have long to wait, otherwise I'd have started a bit of dusting myself, I'm sure I should. Well, as soon as Mrs. Ethelburger came in, you could see that she was in a very bad temper. She didn't even ask me to sit down, so we all three remained standing. I felt so sorry for her husband. He spoke so gently, explaining my visit and everything. I expect I looked a bit upset, not being asked to sit down, or asked about you, for instance. 'What do you want?' she said. That's all. I mean one doesn't have to be conventional and speak about the weather, but there *are* ways of being polite, aren't there? Well, she had the grace to listen, and when Mr. Ethelburger had finished she said, 'If Christopher wants to be confirmed, then it's all right.' 'I am glad you feel that way about it,' I said. She looked so bad-tempered there didn't seem any more to say, and so in order to make my departure I said, 'I hope we shall be seeing one another at the dinner party at the end of the week, then.' 'Yes, we shall be there,' Mr. Ethelburger said, or something like that. And then, in passing, I just let it slip out how sorry I was about the Broom tragedy—what a scandal the woman had caused bringing all that worry on her husband, and of course Mr. Noyce, too, I said, because people will talk. You should have seen Mrs. Ethelburger! She stamped her foot—she shouted—really she did—'Nonsense!' she said. 'It's all absolute nonsense! You're all humbugs! Tragedy and scandal! And what is scandalous, I should like to know, about a woman brave enough to make up her mind to leave? And you call it tragic because her miserable little husband is left snivelling at home. That's tragic, is it? Because he can't nag her any more, can't oppress her, can't worry her into her grave—that's a tragedy for him, you say! And her? What about her? It doesn't strike you that she might be very happy, that life might now be pleasant for her, that she has chosen rightly for herself?' And so on and so on. My dear, it went on and on. It's funny now, frightfully funny—look at me laughing! But it was no joke then, I can tell you. I didn't know where to look. And all the time there was her husband staring down at her so patiently, not saying a word, watching his wife make an absolute fool of herself. Because really, Arthur, I don't suppose for one minute she even knew Mrs. Broom, and certainly was not on friendly terms with her. And what an incredible way to behave in front of a visitor! Fancy allowing one's temper to get the upper hand like that. Naturally when she had finished making an exhibition of herself, which she did quite suddenly, and he just said her name and took her hands—he's much too good for her—what she needs is a real old-fashioned Victorian husband, someone like my father who would never have stood for any such nonsense—when she had come to her senses I naturally pretended she was ill—after all, she may be expecting again—and I said she mustn't upset herself and that I was extremely sorry to have brought up the unpleasant subject, and that of course I would forget at once every word she had said, because it was all nerves. 'I'll let myself out, don't you worry,' I said, because nobody made any move. I thought Mr. Ethelburger might at least have followed me when I went out along the passage, but I suppose he was too overcome by his wife's behaviour to remember the little politenesses. A pity, because I wanted to be able to say to him quietly how very sorry I was about the whole thing, and how much I sympathised with him. Oh really, just think what a life that woman must lead him! A terrible woman. One of those middle-class sluts, I'm afraid, that one reads about so often. Neurotic they are called in novels. Oh dear, what a 'servants' hall story,' as Emm would call it. I simply must put it all in my next letter."

"Yes, you could always do that," the Rector said. "You have a great sense of humour, Clare, and you do love telling a story. But you ought sometimes to allow yourself to feel sad. Sadness and the act of compassion bring people together as much as laughter, you know. And this is a sad story."

"And vulgar—don't you think it's vulgar?" she said.

"Vulgar, common, ordinary, usual—yes. But what is not, for instance?"

"I meant, ill-bred."

"You believe in inherited characteristics, do you, my dear? She shouts because of her middle-class mother, but you, being upper class, laugh?"

"You are making fun of me, Arthur." Mrs. Spark began taking out the socks again.

"No, don't do that," the Rector said. "Whenever you touch those horrible grey things your face puts on a harried, agitated look with all the wrinkles there that are waiting for you in another ten years if you allow the expression to become a habit. Let your hands be idle if it offends you so to use them. I would much rather go about in rags than cause you suffering. Besides, they are beautiful hands. Fold them again and try to be at rest."

Mrs. Spark sighed. "I find it harder and harder growing old," she said; "and I thought it would be so easy. But one doesn't change. Perhaps because I was never very intelligent, I always found things, especially new things, very difficult when I was young. But I always looked forward to an easy, peaceful old age, a golden time when all that had to be done was done and there was no more struggling. About sixty I reckoned that time would come. Well, now at sixty-five I don't believe in it any more. And that leaves an emptiness. There is nothing in the world to hope for any more. I'm sorry. I know this is selfish."

"But one does change," her husband said. "Before Bob died, you would never have felt like that. How a woman can resign herself to the death of her child, I don't know."

"You don't speak like a father," she said. "Or did it mean so little being Bob's father that when he dies you simply bow your head?"

"Do not let us quarrel," the Rector said.

By this time the sun had set, leaving an enormous golden sky that drained all colour from the world and made all things seem small.

"My goodness, what a sunset!" said the Rector. "Oh, Clare, how beautiful it all is—here is your golden age!"

"Do you know what it reminds me of?" she said. "One of those travel films—the end part—'And so we say good-bye to the happy land of so-and-so.' It's just like that."

"But you have no *imagination*, my dear woman!" her husband cried. "Fancy having to quote the cinema when confronted with a vision! Pooh, you old Philistine. Come over here and stand by me. Watch those birds flying homewards in unison, look at the river water disappearing into the horizon—isn't there something enchanted about this evening? Don't you feel the way you are staring there into the distance that something has gone, the embarkation is done, the journey started; and we are left watching and waiting? But we, too, are part of the evening, we are mysterious beings who, although we cannot follow the sun, know that to-morrow it will return."

"Oh dear, oh dear," Mrs. Spark said. "I don't know whether I am supposed to laugh or cry! Really, you are very funny standing there waving your arms about. And wasn't that poetry? You make me feel a bit mean. But grand, too. Mean because I can't help laughing at you, and grand because I am your wife and you do understand so much more than I do. Now, for goodness' sake let's go in. It really is getting damp, and we can go on looking at the sunset through the french windows."

In case you think the Rector is a ridiculous person, I must explain at once that he is a complicated character. To begin with, he was a Senior Wrangler in his time. Then he fell in love with Bach and turned to music, and then, always a religious man, he was at length ordained. When the living in the next-door village to where his father lived fell vacant, he moved in there with his newly wedded wife. And there he still is. He is old, of course, now, at the time of my story, but that is an advantage: he knows everybody. He christened Mr. Ethelburger, he was there when nurse, in spite of her Baptist denomination, took the little Noyces to church with their mother and father. And long afterwards he would sit listening by the hour while old Mrs. Noyce talked about her absent son. He very seldom visits people unless invited to do so, but whoever goes to him is welcomed in at any time; indeed, none of the doors of his house is ever locked. Mr. Browning is his friend, and even Mrs. Browning likes him. He once sat for Mrs. Noyce, and put her in touch with some University friends of his who bought the portrait; so there is a certain bond between himself and Mrs. Noyce, although they hardly ever meet. And in a way he knows all about Mr. Browning and Mrs. Ethelburger. It happened like this. The Rector and his wife used to take a short holiday together sometimes in Knightsbridge with Mrs. Spark's sister Emm. (The one Mrs. Spark was always writing to, a fierce old lady who wore black bonnets and cackled even in her sleep. But you don't have to meet her, as she does not ever come into this story.) One morning, rather early, Mr. Spark was out exercising Emm's little dog. He was going along towards the park, when he suddenly saw two familiar figures standing by a shop window, looking in. He was just about to call out "Hullo! Fancy meeting you here!" when he checked himself. After all, it *was* early; none of the shops was open yet; and Mrs. Ethelburger was leaning on Mr. Browning's arm. He remembered then that she was supposed to be staying in Wales with a friend, and that Mr. Browning was sent away by his firm on urgent business, he had said. So the Rector picked up Emm's little dog and went by another way to the park.

Familiarity does not always breed contempt; obviously not, or no two people or groups of people would ever find a peaceful way of living together, but the Rector, who had lived all these years surrounded by the same little group, found a certain bitterness, a sad detachment, creeping into his relations with some of those about him. A regular attendance at church may not have signified any deep religious feeling, but at least it had brought everyone together once a week to be disciplined by the same ritual. Now fewer and fewer people came to church, some never coming at all, or only on the occasion of a marriage or for the burial service. At the death of old Mr. Noyce, the Rector had found himself removed as it were from a central position among his flock. The new Mr. Noyce sold up a large part of his father's estate (it was bought by the retired owner of a chain of grocery stores, who built himself a Tudor mansion and lived in seclusion on the borders of the parish), and there were no more village entertainments at the Manor. In a material sense the loss of old Mr. Noyce had made little difference to the village people; those who had been dismissed from the Noyce estate found work with the retired grocer, and their children, who might otherwise have found local employment, went into the town five miles away, where they got jobs in the carpet factory with better pay than their fathers. But in another sense, in the language of ideas, they lost a figurehead. Every loss is painful to some degree, even though it has no material importance. The Rector had none of the attributes of leadership; he had neither the character, the status nor the time-honoured name that had held old Mr. Noyce safe in his magical position, and while the two together had appeared to be as independent equals like the State and the Church, when the old Squire died the old order died with him and the Rector was left behind. Gradually the church became empty. Later on, with a brave indifference to the facts, Mr. Browning took it upon himself to be a sort of part-time leader. His work claimed him during the week, but at week-ends and in the holidays when he was free, he spent endless trouble organising village socials (games of cards with penny cups of tea, dances and competitions) and various village fetes.

"My flock," the Rector sometimes called them.

"Your sheep," Mr. Browning said.

All this made it more difficult than ever for the Rector. Organised entertainment does not necessarily put people in a religious or even a church-going frame of mind. And, in any case, left to itself the village was in a good way to finding its own entertainment. Sport—cricket and football—was what brought the young men together. Village boys do not think much of cards, tea-drinking or even dancing, and village girls like to watch their young men beat the visiting cricket or football team. But the Rector had never been much good at sport. How could he enter into the life of his flock? It puzzled him. And then, talking the matter over with his wife one evening in the boathouse by the river, he had had an idea.

"It's no good my paying visits to the Noyces' when they never come to church," Mrs. Spark had just said.

"My dear," the Rector said, "those sort of people no longer have any importance. Don't visit them if you don't like them."

His wife was rather horrified.

"Well, the Ethelburgers have lived here for a long time, of course," she said.

"I shouldn't bother about that sort of visit any more," he said. "Do you know what I'm going to do, Clare? I'm going to be consulted like a doctor. It shouldn't be so difficult. I know everyone. I know the sort of troubles that afflict them. I can help them, if only they will come to me."

All this was some time ago, and since then the Rector has had many new ideas (the latest is gardening), but on the whole his work has been successful; he loves his people and is liked by them. However, there is this feeling of bitterness I have mentioned. The Rector, whose face is mild and kind, does not look on everyone with the same degree of affection. And sometimes when not in a loving mood he says things like, "There are some I could mention"; or, "I name no names," in contexts which leave little doubt as to the offender—generally Mr. Noyce. His wife apes this oblique method of attack in conversation, and, as you have seen, in letters.

Well, it is late now; the sun has long ago sunk down, and the Rector is watching his wife play patience by the fireside.

"Black nine on red ten," he says.

She ignores him and puts up the ace of spades.

Suddenly the bell rings. She looks at the clock.

"Half-past nine. Who ever can that be?" she says.

"You'd better let me go," the Rector says.

He puts the black nine on the red ten in passing.

"If it's someone to see you, don't let them keep you up late," Mrs. Spark says. "I'm just going to finish this off, then I'm going to bed."

It was someone to see the Rector, it was Mrs. Darlington, Linda's mother.

Mrs. Spark jumped up and opened the drawing-room door an inch or two directly after her husband disappeared down the passage. That way she could see if he let anyone in at the front door. She saw who it was and went back to her game of patience. It came out in about five minutes' time, so she dealt herself another. That, too, came out. She looked at the clock. "Ten minutes more," she said; "the woman must have finished by then."

Ten minutes passed and still Mrs. Darlington had not gone. So Mrs. Spark went out into the kitchen and made some tea. Then she went to the study door, knocked, and without waiting for an answer, went in. "Oh, good evening, Mrs. Darlington," she said, raising her eyebrows. "Excuse me, I was just bringing the Rector his nightcap."

"Thank you, my dear. Put it down, will you? Thank you," he said. He poured the tea out when she had gone. There was only one cup. He offered this to Mrs. Darlington, who would not accept it. "But you must," the Rector said; "isn't this just the time for a cup of tea?"

"I'm sure I don't know," Mrs. Darlington said. She took it, however.

"Well now, let me just think a bit," the Rector said. He took out his pipe and filled it and lit it. He tipped his chair backwards away from the table.

"The trouble is," he said after a bit, "I have no say with the young people. I know the White girls, Dorothy and Pat, of course. Nice girls. I suppose Linda isn't friendly with them, by any chance?"

"No. She's got no friends," Mrs. Darlington said. "That's what's always worried me." She stirred and stirred her tea.

"You don't think the whole thing is nonsense out of her head?" the Rector said.

"No, Sir. A young girl doesn't go making those sort of things up." She went on stirring.

"Now, do drink that tea," the Rector said. "I should think the best thing for you to do, in any case, Mrs. Darlington, is to write to Mrs. Noyce and say that your daughter is needed at home. And don't let her go up there any more, if you are really worried."

"Oh, but I've done that," she said. "She just writes back to me that she's having a party Saturday and can't let Linda go. I brought the letter along with me. Here it is."

The Rector waved it aside.

"Tell Linda she is *not* to go," he said.

"Well, I *could* do," Mrs. Darlington said. She sipped her tea.

"Do you know," the Rector said, "I believe Linda is just a naughty little girl and made the whole story up because you hurt her feelings when you said it was time she started collecting for her bottom drawer instead of moping about the place. Has she a quick temper?"

"Very quick," Mrs. Darlington said, "she gets that from her father. But the way she turned on me in a flash, tossing her head—'Keep your old bottom drawer to yourself. Mum!' she came out with. 'If you think I'm after one of them village boys, you've made a mistake. See? I've got something a long way better than that up at the Manor.' It took me a while to figure it out what she meant. Then I says, 'Linda, whatever are you talking about?' And then she says what I told you."

"That Mr. Noyce carries on with her in the airing cupboard. It doesn't really sound very probable," the Rector said. "What do you think she meant exactly by 'carrying on,' Mrs. Darlington?"

"We—ell," Mrs. Darlington said, sliding her eyes from side to side.

"I see," the Rector said.

She finished her tea. "It's ever so nice of you to help—I'm sure we shall be all right now that I've spoken," she said.

"Well, keep it to yourself now. Don't speak to anyone else," the Rector said.

He sat alone for a while after she had gone, shaking his head. "Impossible—or is it possible?" he murmured to himself. But when, later, he met his wife on the landing and told her the whole story before going to bed, she refused to take the matter at all seriously.

"Rubbish!" she said. "The whole thing is a farce. Somebody is pulling your leg."

He rebuked her, saying, "Village people are not frivolous. When they bring me their troubles, I take a serious view of their affairs."

"Well, all I can say is," she said, "much as I dislike Mr. Noyce, and we know quite a lot of nasty things about him—the airing cupboard! No, Arthur. Somebody's trying to be funny."

"I do wish you wouldn't always *laugh*," the Rector said.

CHAPTER SIX

LET us go at once to the Manor and see about this pairing cupboard. The cupboard itself is an enormous and suffocating place, heated by coils of pipes connected with the bath-water system. The lowest shelf, being the most convenient, is stacked with household linen, clean underwear and various sizes of blankets which are stored there during the summer. All these things are in use, although there are so many sheets it might take several months of weekly changes for this household to get through them in rotation. But on the top shelf, for which there is a small step-ladder kept right at the bottom of the cupboard together with an old pair of boots, picture frames and all sorts of other dusty and forgotten things, on the top shelf there are pillows and eiderdowns from the beds in the house which are never used; and these, stacked in a tidy pile, the pillows at one side, the eiderdowns at the other, form a sort of couch reaching almost up to the ceiling. So much for the actual cupboard. But the cupboard is in a room between two landings. One door leads straight down the back stairway and is kept locked from the inside because nurse thinks the stairs are dangerous just there, and the other door opens on to a long passage with empty bedrooms all down one side and a number of high, small windows opposite, on which lost bluebottles bump and buzz in summer. This passage leads eventually to a baize door, connecting the servants' quarters—the empty bedrooms, empty because both nurse and cook are far too old to climb up all those stairs—with the landing of the front staircase. Thus, when you come to think of it, the airing cupboard is not such a bad place, after all, in which to conduct a surreptitious love affair. And it was here that Linda worked two mornings a week, ironing by the long window opposite the cupboard, quite by herself.

But nurse and Mrs. Noyce are up there to-day doing the ironing.

"It does seem a lot of unnecessary work, all this," Mrs. Noyce was saying.

"In the old days we never had electric irons," nurse said.

"You must help me find someone else from the village," said Mrs. Noyce. "I don't know what we shall do about the party at the end of the week. Unless we just have a cold supper. But really, we must find someone else. What's the matter with old Mrs. Darlington wanting her daughter home in such a hurry? I can't understand. It's so inconsiderate. Or do you think Linda wanted to leave all the time, in spite of the protests and the tears? But she was such a nice girl, I thought. Quiet, and she never made any trouble. You can never tell though, what goes on inside people's heads."

"And just as well," nurse said.

Mrs. Noyce frowned, but went on with the ironing. "Well," she said, "what about getting somebody else?"

"Mrs. Walmby's the one to ask, not me," nurse said. "I don't have anything to do with the village nowadays."

"So you are not going to help, Nurse?"

"Oh, pardon me—you know as well as I do, I do all in my power to help Mr. Noyce and yourself." Mrs. Noyce laughed. "Now, now, Nurse," she said. "I know you disapprove of me, but you mustn't always put on that tone of voice when you speak to me. Otherwise there'll be trouble—I shall make a scene and refuse to be bullied—or something dreadful like that. Let's keep it friendly."

"Hearing you talk that way reminds me of someone else, it does indeed," nurse said. She took the shirt Mrs. Noyce had just finished ironing and hung it over a towel-horse.

"Who?" Mrs. Noyce said quietly.

"I know you didn't mean to be rude, Miss Eileen; so please don't think I have forgotten my manners if I say when you spoke to me then you reminded me very much of Linda."

"Really? And when did you talk to Linda? You had to reprove her about something, I suppose."

"I did," nurse said. "You see, Miss Eileen, sitting there upstairs painting all day as you do, you don't know anything that goes on in the house."

"Oh dear," said Mrs. Noyce. "I do wish you'd tell me what you are going to tell me if you want to, Nurse, without all these dreadful hints. Otherwise I shall imagine you caught the master and Linda kissing in the shrubbery or something. You've made a nasty feel about the place, or perhaps it's always frowsty and unnatural up here. Anyway, you will please tell me what you mean."

"And I will, too," nurse said. "It didn't take me long, Miss Eileen, to see that Linda Darlington was making eyes at the master, the wicked girl. Such a nice girl, you say, so quiet, never made any trouble! I shouldn't be surprised if we had a great deal of trouble coming to us the way things have happened. Goodness knows what she has been telling her mother, the little liar. And you say she never made any trouble. It all came from shutting yourself up, Miss Eileen. It's not for me to say, but it doesn't seem fair on poor Master Harry."

"Finish the ironing, will you please, Nurse," Mrs. Noyce said. "I'm sorry, but this happens to be just the sort of thing I can't stand. It's mean and it's silly and it's a damn waste of time." She walked towards the door. It was the locked one, so she couldn't get out all at once.

"Stop a minute, stop, Miss Eileen!" called nurse.

"Why is this door locked—I never locked it. Oh! it's all ridiculous," Mrs. Noyce said. "I don't care what people do behind my back—I'm going to get on with my painting." She turned the key in the lock as nurse was saying "Not that way—not that way, Miss Eileen, it's dangerous!"

"You make me furious!" Mrs. Noyce said, going out. And she fell down the stairs.

"There! There now—what did I say?" the old woman cried out, moving heavily after her mistress. She almost tripped over the flex and the iron toppled over on to some clothes as she went out, groping and calling, "Are you hurt? Oh, don't say you've broken anything! Oh, whatever will Master Harry have to say about all this?"

Mrs. Noyce was not very badly hurt. She had saved herself by falling against the banisters. She allowed nurse to take her arm, and like this she hobbled along to her room one flight farther down, where nurse examined her ankle, which was a bit swollen. By the time cold compresses had been put on and the ankle was bandaged, a smell of something burning had already seeped down to that part of the house.

"Nasty smell," Mrs. Noyce said, sniffing.

"Now you just keep lying down for a bit. It's a bonfire, I daresay. You don't have to bother your head about that," nurse said.

Mrs. Walmby was frying onions for lunch and noticed nothing. And Mr. Noyce was down in the cellar trying to make up his mind as to what sort of wine to have for the dinner party at the end of the week.

Mr. Broom was in the apple orchard looking up at the trees. He noticed a lot of smoke piling up in the sky and walked out into the open to see what it was all about. Immediately he saw the house was on fire he ran through the garden gate shouting the gardener's name as he went, but not stopping to find out whether his shouts had been heard. The gardener was in the potting-shed, and poked his head out of the window when he heard his name called. And then he, too, saw the smoke. By this time Mr. Broom had reached the kitchen door. He ran into the kitchen. But as soon as Mrs. Walmby saw him she said, "Here! What do you think you're doing in my kitchen with dirty boots on!"

"Your house is on fire, my good woman," Mr. Broom said.

She stared at him with the frying-pan in one hand and a knife in the other.

"Where's the master and mistress?" Mr. Broom said, and without waiting for an answer, went off to find them himself. The gardener and his boy arrived just then with buckets from the potting-shed, and Mrs. Walmby suddenly came to life.

"Fire! Fire!" she shouted, dropping the frying-pan on the table. "Fire! Mr. Broom says there's a fire! Oh dear, whatever am I going to do?"

The gardener handed her a bucket and led the way up the back stairs.

Meanwhile, Mrs. Noyce played her part. She first of all rang up the fire brigade and then ordered nurse and Mrs. Walmby out of the house.

"I don't know where your master is," she said; "he's probably out for a walk or something, but you might go round outside calling through the windows. Only you are not to come in the house, understand? Otherwise you'll get burnt to death."

Mrs. Walmby snatched the gong from its place at the bottom of the stairs as she went, and once outside began beating it, hard. In spite of her swollen ankle, Mrs. Noyce ran upstairs very quickly and shouted to the gardener and his boy and Mr. Broom to come down. They were throwing water from their buckets into the smoke, which came in suffocating billows down the stairs.

"The fire extinguishers—help me with the fire extinguishers!" Mrs. Noyce said.

But when they had lifted them down from the shelves, nobody knew how they worked.

Suddenly Mr. Noyce appeared, carrying two bottles of wine in each hand.

"My dear, what on earth has happened?" he said.

"Come on, give us a hand with these—the house is on fire," Mrs. Noyce said.

"On *fire*?"

"Yes, we're on fire, Sir. Upstairs in the airing cupboard, I reckon," Mr. Broom said. "Better not waste time."

Mr. Noyce put down the wine bottles, carefully, on the shelf where the fire extinguishers had been.

"Has that girl been upstairs ironing?" he said.

"She's left, I told you at breakfast, she's left," Mrs. Noyce said. "I did the ironing."

"Well, is the iron still on?" Mr. Noyce said.

"Oh!" said Mrs. Noyce, clapping a hand on her chest.

"Go and turn the electricity off at the main—you know where it is?" Mr. Noyce said. And picking up a fire extinguisher, "Come on, you," he said to the others, "I've always wanted to know if these things really worked."

They did work. They worked so well that, attacked from the main staircase side of the house where there was less smoke, the fire died down and was eventually extinguished. The gardener and boy and Mr. Broom were standing about and Mr. Noyce was grumbling and kicking the mess when the fire brigade arrived. Mrs. Noyce ran up to tell them. "Who the hell summoned the fire brigade?" Mr. Noyce said.

"I did," said his wife.

They looked at one another in silence.

"Well, we'll be getting along," Mr. Broom said, signalling with his thumb to the gardener.

"You women—really!" Mr. Noyce said, after they had gone. "I only have to turn my back one moment, and the house is on fire!"

"Don't be so ridiculous, Harry," Mrs. Noyce said. "If I hadn't fallen downstairs, it would never have happened."

"What on earth's the matter with you all?" Mr. Noyce began. But at that moment the first of the firemen arrived along the passage, walking carefully and bending his head because the ceiling was low and he had his helmet on.

"It's all over. It's out," Mr. Noyce said, stepping aside so that the man could see.

CHAPTER SEVEN

Mrs. Spark is very concerned about Linda. Her husband warns of the dangers of interference, but the feeling inside her that something ought to be done compels her to act. So after breakfast one morning when the Rector has shut himself up in his study, she leaves Mrs. White in charge of the house with a list of instructions about answering doorbells, how much bread to take from the baker, how much tea to put in the pot for herself and the Rector at eleven o'clock if she (Mrs. Spark) isn't back, and the number of rooms to be cleaned, and those rooms which are certainly not to be cleaned, and some last-minute advice about the boiler which is supposed to use anthracite but has had to be fuelled with coke and is apt to burn itself out. After all this, Mrs. Spark sets off down the drive with a firm expression on her face. She holds a little purse in one hand and a pale grey stick with a band of silver round it near the top in the other. She has pinned her hat on very firmly because of the wind, and walks firmly but not too fast, using the stick to knock chestnuts and other bits of rubbish off the path out of the way. There is a splendid avenue of chestnut trees from the house to the Rectory gates. But Mrs. Spark is in the road outside now. She keeps her eyes fixed on somewhere ahead, and does not look in the direction of the council houses or the thatched cottages which stand behind their gardens each side of the road. If anyone says "Good morning," she says "Good morning" and passes on.

Here she is, then, staring at the brass knocker on the Darlingtons' door, waiting for an answer. Mrs. Darlington opens the door. She has her carpet slippers on and wipes her fingers on a very dirty old apron.

"Good morning," she says.

"Good morning. I wonder if I could have a little talk with you," Mrs. Spark says.

They talk in the parlour, where it is at once cold and airless; a neutral sort of place that, nevertheless, has character. Here there are vases without flowers and many chairs with plump upholstered seats which have never succumbed to the human anatomy, and a black-leaded grate, with the fire-irons arranged criss-cross before it, where no fire burns. There are pictures over the mantelpiece and a grey portrait of a wedding hangs over the doorway. It is exceptionally clean and dustless in here, and rather dark because of the complicated arrangement of the net curtains. "Fear thy God" says a plate on the mantelpiece. It is not a comfortable place.

Mrs. Spark is, of course, talking about Linda. She has said many times already that it is for her own good, but all to no purpose. Mrs. Darlington just shakes her head and says it would never do with Linda. The trouble is, Mrs. Spark has come armed with a plan, and Mrs. Darlington, who has always just managed somehow, is defending her way of life as well as her daughter. I am not going to tell you the whole conversation in detail, but the crux of the matter is that Mrs. Spark thinks it high time Linda was harnessed to doing something useful, and as the factories in the town are crying out for unskilled workers, Linda should get a job in the town, going in by bus every morning and back at night, as many of the other village girls do. But Mrs. Darlington says no, that way Linda would come to despise her home, like Julie and Freda who were good girls before they learnt how to doll themselves up, paint their faces and go to the cinema. And besides, all that way off from home with nobody to keep an eye on her, Linda would be bound to get herself into trouble. Serious trouble. No, it would never do with Linda.

You may think I am making an unnecessary fuss about Linda, that anyway she is an impossible character, and that now, thank goodness, she doesn't work at the Manor any more, and there need be no more bother about her, and all I've got to do is to get on with the story. I know how you feel. But in a small community like this village, any individual who makes a commotion affects the rest. I cannot show you everyone, but I assure you everyone has his importance as the hills have their importance, or the weeds, when looking at the scenery.

Linda lives in a world of her own that bears even less resemblance than usual to what is casually referred to as the 'real' world; meaning, I suppose, the rather unpleasant place one wakes up to on Monday when the alarm goes off and there's no chance of another five minutes in bed. It's quite a long time since Mr. Noyce smiled absent-mindedly at Linda in the garden, but because of her peculiar reaction, the consequences of that smile have had power to activate my story. Or do you think that, in any case, the airing cupboard would have been set on fire and that things happen like ripe pears falling down in autumn? Yes, there is an autumn for everything. But there is no need to feel tied down, because there is nothing personal about autumn, and the general idea if you turn to Nature for an interpretation, is to get a move on. So much for autumn, then. And there is no need to worry about the airing cupboard, because the fire there did no great harm, in fact, like so many things in the past, it taught everyone a lesson. Up at the Manor they are all very busy interpreting that lesson just now.

"The thing is," Mr. Noyce is saying, walking up and down with a bite of ham-sandwich in his mouth, "the thing is, Eileen, that you have no proper sense of responsibility. I mean, even though you are an artist and must paint, still you've got to live somewhere. And because it was as much your choice as mine that we should live here and not sell this place, I do feel you can't treat it just like a cave or something that hides you from the weather. You've simply got to take a more positive interest in the way this place is run, Eileen. It's no good falling downstairs in a temper and setting the place on fire because nurse tells you things you ought to have noticed for yourself. And if you want a girl in from the village or someone, it's no good giving vague instructions to other people. You've got to find the girl yourself." He took another bite out of the ham-sandwich and sat down.

Mrs. Noyce watched the smoke from her cigarette. "Why don't you?" she said.

"Me?" said Mr. Noyce. "Good heavens! I mean—well really, Eileen."

"Words fail you," she said. "But, after all, you are more likely to know better than me the sort of person who won't make eyes at you—which was the cause of all the trouble."

"I think you might be serious about this."

"I am serious. Only I do wish you wouldn't always lecture me."

Mr. Noyce took another ham-sandwich from the table. "I do hate these semi-picnic lunches," he said. "Can't we have a proper meal at lunch sometimes?"

"Yes, if you make it yourself. Mrs. Walmby can't manage two proper meals a day. Besides, if you insist on a dinner party, she's got to prepare for it," Mrs. Noyce said.

Mr. Noyce banged the table with his free hand. Everything rattled. There was a silence. Then he said, "It's come to this. When I speak to you, you say I am giving you a lecture, so you don't listen. How, then, are we going to communicate?"

"Well, if you got down off your high horse on to a more human level, it might help," Mrs. Noyce said.

"On any human level you'd have had a plate chucked at you long ago," he said. "But look here, Eileen, I refuse to quarrel. The thing is, you've got to take time off from painting to get things straight. We can't go on like this. I can't do everything."

So that afternoon Mrs. Noyce put on her cloak (it was rather a cold day) and went off down to the village. First of all she called in at the post-office. Mr. Blonsom was serving.

"I expect you know Linda Darlington has left me. Do you know anyone else who would come and work at the Manor?" Mrs. Noyce asked him. She had rather large eyes and a habit of watching people, not curiously, but with a sort of melancholy indifference. The effect of this on Mr. Blonsom was to make him behave as though he were guilty. He blushed and dropped a packet of envelopes, and then when she continued to look at him, called out to his wife, "Con, Mrs. Noyce here wants to see you," and retreated behind a screen at the back of the shop.

"Yes?" said Mrs. Blonsom, appearing suddenly.

"Sorry to disturb you," Mrs. Noyce said, "but I thought you might know of someone who would come and work for me. Linda has left, you know."

"Has?" Mrs. Blonsom said. Her eyes were rather large, too.

"Perhaps if you don't know anyone, you know someone who could help me. Because you must know everyone here, don't you?" Mrs. Noyce said.

"I do know most," Mrs. Blonsom said, scratching an elbow. "I was sorry to hear you'd had trouble up at the Manor. We saw the fire-engine. I hope there isn't a great deal of damage."

"No, not much really," said Mrs. Noyce. "But about this girl—someone to help, I mean—"

"You might try Mrs. Spark at the Rectory," Mrs. Blonsom said, "she knows a lot about people in the village."

Mrs. Spark still had her hat on from that morning's outing. She sat Mrs. Noyce down by the sitting-room fire in the comfortable chair, and perched herself opposite with her back to the light. "You don't mind if I get on with my mending, do you?" she said. "I was so sorry to hear about all your troubles. And it must have been terrible, that fire."

"Oh, one gets over these things," Mrs. Noyce said. She then explained her visit.

"Very sensible of you to come. I was wondering whether you would," Mrs. Spark said.

"Then you do know someone?" Mrs. Noyce said, looking up into the light.

"Oh, good gracious no, I didn't mean that," said Mrs. Spark. "You can be quite frank with me, you know. The Rector and I both think Linda behaved disgracefully." She looked down over her work at Mrs. Noyce. Mrs. Noyce looked into the fire.

"I had no idea people gossiped so much," she said. "It's a sort of cliché that everyone knows what everyone else is doing in a village. Well, I hate that sort of thing. I think all intrigue and back-biting is foul. I think when people have to live together they ought to try to live decently. I don't know how Linda behaved, I refuse to listen to such stupid gossip. To tell you the truth, I still don't know why she left. Other people have had a great deal to tell me, but she herself never said anything. But the point is, she has gone now, and I'm looking for somebody else."

Mrs. Spark smiled over her darning. "You see, Mrs. Noyce," she said, "you won't get anyone else. It's hard enough to get people to work these days even in the best of jobs. But after this, and everyone knows what has happened, if you see what I mean, I'm afraid no one is going to offer themselves for work at the Manor."

"Oh well, in that case I won't waste any more of my time," Mrs. Noyce said, getting up.

"Don't go now! Don't go! Why, you've only just arrived," Mrs. Spark cried. "Let us talk this thing over. Surely two sensible women like ourselves ought to be able to put this nonsense straight. And I agree with you, Mrs. Noyce, *how* I agree," she said putting out a hand, "about the vulgarity and beastliness of gossip."

Mrs. Noyce had already drawn her cloak about her, but she hesitated then. "You don't like me because I am an artist," she said. "You think I have nothing to do all day long but just sit around, don't you? It's a very common mistake. Two sensible women like ourselves, you say, but do you think I'm a sensible woman?"

Mrs. Spark put out both her hands. "Dear Mrs. Noyce," she said, "now please do sit down. I can't answer all those questions in this position—I shall get a crick in the neck. And please do forgive me for being personal when I say what a wonderful colour that cloak is! Only an artist would dare to have chosen that colour."

Mrs. Noyce looked down at her cloak. "Yes, it is nice. I'm fond of crimson," she said.

Of course she sat down again in the end, and Mrs. Spark rang the bell and asked Mrs. White to make tea.

"You are such an elusive person, you know," Mrs. Spark was saying while they drank their tea; "honestly, you are a stranger. And much as one would like to get to know you, one doesn't know how to start. That's why we are all so excited about the party. I think it's wonderful of you to have it, after all; what with the fire and all this other trouble."

"Why should anyone want to know me? Only because I'm an artist and they think that queer," Mrs. Noyce said.

"Not at all," Mrs. Spark said. "You have no idea how lonely people really are. Look at me, for instance, I've loved having you here. And there's poor Mrs. Ethelburger up at the farm. Who has she got to be friends with? You know, I think we all have a certain duty towards each other, to get to know one another."

"Oh, we know Mrs. Ethelburger," Mrs. Noyce said. "I should have thought she had enough to do with all those children and the farm, without feeling lonely."

"And dear Mr. Ethelburger, he does so adore her."

"Does he?" Mrs. Noyce asked, looking across at Mrs. Spark, fixing her with her large eyes.

"Oh yes, good gracious me," Mrs. Spark said. She looked away and sighed.

"Oh," Mrs. Noyce said.

"I suppose you, being an artist, must be very interested in people," Mrs. Spark said. "I mean, well, from your point of view Mrs. Ethelburger must be an exceptionally interesting person, I should think."

"I don't quite know what you mean," Mrs. Noyce said.

"Oh, come now," Mrs. Spark said. "She is so beautiful, and such an emotional person. You must have noticed that, if you know her."

"I don't really know her. I don't know anyone here well," Mrs. Noyce said.

"Now that's just what I'm driving at," Mrs. Spark said. "You have cut yourself off away there up at the Manor, honestly you have. Do you know, I always thought you were a rather dreadful, sulky sort of person before to-day, when I have begun to get to know you, if I may say so. And look, you are not at all like that! It has been most interesting, *most* interesting, having you to talk to. I understand now something of what it means to be an artist. Oh, only something! But you are no longer a stranger, someone who hardly counts but is rather a nuisance. I mean you don't come to church and that sort of thing. Perhaps you never will. Never mind. The thing is, I have had a chance to know you and to try to understand. I see now, it's very difficult for you. You are a serious person, you believe you have something to do, something that matters. Well, I don't know anything about painting, but listening to you and watching your face while you talk about your work has given me something to think about. I've always been interested in careers for women, but at the same time I have always thought careers so silly if there is a home to be run and a husband to look after and all the rest of it. Now, I'm not suggesting that you come and speak to my women at the Women's Institute! But I do think many other people would be interested, like me. And I do urge you to have a little more to do with the village—it might even help with your painting!"

"Well, it's very nice of you to put it like that. And fancy bothering to listen to me all this time! My husband says I always talk too much, given the chance," Mrs. Noyce said.

"I tell you what," said Mrs. Spark, "when you have the time, you might just go round to Mrs. Ethelburger, if you haven't been there, and ask her whether you couldn't borrow her girl for the party. Or perhaps her girl might know another one. That's how it works, you know."

Yes, things can work that way. There goes Mrs. Noyce, a tall person wrapped in a billowing crimson cloak, battling against the east wind as she walks up the drive to the farm. And here is Mr. Ethelburger, feeling hungry (he hasn't yet had his tea), coming in from the fields.

"Who the hell . . ." Mr. Ethelburger says to himself.

They meet.

"Oh, how do you do?" he says. "I won't shake hands. Look at me, I'm filthy. What are you doing up here? You're such a stranger."

"How do you do," Mrs. Noyce says. "I was just coming up to bother your wife. Mrs. Spark thinks she might be able to help me."

They reach the door.

"Come along in," he says.

The wind blows the door wide open out of Mr. Ethelburger's hands; a tall vase caught in the draught, sways and then crashes to the floor, spilling the flowers and the water all over the place. The dogs stand guard in the hall, barking, and the children cry out from the stairs: "Look! Red Riding Hood! Red Riding Hood!"

Mrs. Ethelburger comes running along the passage with her hair all untidy. There is an extraordinary confusion. And then everyone begins to behave in the proper way.

"Oh, Mrs. Noyce—how nice," Mrs. Ethelburger said. "Children, stop being silly and come and be introduced!"

Mr. Ethelburger shut the door and began mopping up the mess on the floor with a duster.

"Not that," Mrs. Ethelburger said. "Wait a minute, I'll call mother. Do stop those dogs barking."

Everyone seemed entirely self-possessed. And because she was the visitor, nobody took any notice when Mrs. Noyce said, "Please, please! I must go at once—I didn't mean to disturb you—I had no idea—I must get home, I really must!"

And it was taken for granted that she was just being polite when she said, "But I've *had* my tea."

"Well then, come along and have another," Mr. Ethelburger said good-naturedly.

*

It is night now; not very late, but the Rector has gone to bed, tired out after digging in the garden. Mrs. Spark is in her own little room, her sanctuary, pouring out her thoughts to Emm.

"Such an interesting day," she is writing. "First of all, I paid a visit to the Darlingtons—you remember, Emm dear, I told you about our village scandal in my last. I feel quite strongly about that girl. For one thing, it's not right that someone of her age should be left at a loose end when everywhere you look there is so much work to do. And I don't approve of young girls being put to domestic work these days. One should see the thing from their point of view. There is no future in it, and if they want a job with good pay and something to look forward to if they don't get married, I can't think of anything better than our local factory. Local, I say, but anyone would think it's about a thousand miles away the fuss Mrs. Darlington made when I suggested it. In fact, it's about five miles away. I know I am a bit unconventional, but really, these village people live in the dark ages! The poor woman seemed to imagine that her daughter lived in a state of innocence, and that any contact with town life was bound to upset her morals! As if in any case she had not been cinema-fed from the first—otherwise how on earth could she have such sloppy ideas in her head about her employer? Or are we to believe that where there is smoke there is fire? (By the way, it didn't do any damage, I'll explain just how I know in a minute.) But seriously, I do think it wrong that a girl like Linda should be allowed to go about in idleness. Potato picking and such-like are, after all, only casual jobs, and a girl like that needs very careful watching and a lot of hard work with hard discipline if she isn't to go altogether to the bad. None of this made sense of course, to her mother—a tired, little selfish old woman—very cut up about the whole thing, one gathered, but obstinate, oh, how obstinate! I told her she must be very careful not to spread stories in the village, both for her own sake and her daughter's, and that personally I thought her daughter was a little liar. She looked so entirely unhappy when I said this that it crossed my mind—perhaps really she would *like* you-know-who to be caught kissing her daughter in the airing cupboard! These village people are so strange and primitive. I'm afraid my visit was useless.

"But now about my *visitor*. Who should call this afternoon but Mrs. Noyce! You know, Emm, I do sometimes feel that, after all, it's fun being alive. Things are so different, so unexpected, and not at all the sort of shape you thought at first. Mrs. Noyce isn't dreary and arty and impossible—she's rather a human person. And most interesting about her work. What a pity we have never had the chance to talk before, because always when I met her before it was some sort of formal occasion. She talked and talked and talked. I gathered from little things she let drop—'Of course my husband says' and 'Well, I don't think my husband'—you know the sort of thing—that the Noyces don't see eye to eye about everything. In fact, I'm willing to bet he is an absolute brute to her! Please don't think she is a poor little thing—as you know, I am not a bit sentimental, and besides she is a tall, rather important-looking person. But here is someone with a real object in life, with a real feeling that she has a job to do and must get it done—and she has a man like Mr. Noyce for a husband. Arthur, you know, always said she could paint. You remember . . ."

But here Mrs. Spark puts down her pen. Perhaps the day has been too much for her, or perhaps, as it sometimes does happen, the necessary vitality is lacking directly after an exciting encounter for one to be able to make it exciting when writing it down. She reads what she has written and shakes her head. "What will Emm think of me? I'm not a bit like that, really," she says. "What a muddle!"

Mrs. Noyce, on the other hand, didn't look a bit as though she had anything on her mind. She was gay, she laughed, and she wouldn't settle down with a book after dinner, but kept on moving around, rearranging the flowers and passing remarks. Mr. Noyce noticed this.

"Extraordinary you women are," he said. "Just because you've done what I suggested for once and been successful at it, you come home a different person—happy and smiling. Is this girl such a jewel, then? Can't you bribe her to stay if she makes you so happy?"

"Oh, you mean Irene," Mrs. Noyce said. "Yes, it's nice of Mrs. Ethelburger to let me have Irene for the party. But of course she can't stay."

"Tell me, I've often wondered," said Mr. Noyce, "what is that household like? What sort of children have those two produced? And what is *he* like? Do you know, I can't even remember his face."

"Oh, they're all right," Mrs. Noyce said.

"Come on, Eileen, you must have noticed a bit more than that!" her husband said.

"Oh, Harry, I forgot to tell you about the Rector's wife—such a peculiar old woman," said Mrs. Noyce. "You know, she's a terrible old gossip. We talked for hours and hours—all about painting. I kept to that because one has to be careful with these village people. They are always wanting to get personal, you know. She told me, amongst other things, that Mrs. Ethelburger's husband worshipped the ground she trod on. Do you think that's true?"

"How on earth should I know," Mr. Noyce said. "Did she let anything drop about me? I hope you didn't."

"Well, it's been quite fun to-day," said Mrs. Noyce. "It's given me ideas. I think I shall do some more portraits."

"For goodness' sake, don't bring the village here," Mr. Noyce said.

CHAPTER EIGHT

IT IS Wednesday now, and Saturday is the day fixed for the party. Imagine Mrs. Walmby's feelings, then, when her mistress appears in the kitchen just after breakfast, and calmly informs her that she has found someone to help on Saturday.

"It's not that we don't need help here, but whoever's said we couldn't manage Saturday?" Mrs. Walmby said to nurse afterwards over their morning cup of tea. "It's not even being asked, never being consulted, that turns me wild. And then to have Mrs. Ethelburger's Irene, just like that! 'I'm ever so sorry, Ma'am,' I says, 'but I can't have strangers in my kitchen Saturday.' She looks at me hard the way she does. 'Cook, what's the matter with Irene?' she says. 'Oh, I've nothing against the girl, I'm sure,' I says. 'She's idle, she's bone lazy, but it's nothing to do with that. Why didn't you ask me, Ma'am, if you thought I couldn't manage,' I says. Then she says something about the Master. That's right, I thinks to meself, blame him! But I say nothing, I stand there with me mouth shut, holding my peace till she goes. If you want my opinion, the whole thing is balmy. Parties was all right in the old days, but now what's the good of a party when nobody entertains?"

Mr. Noyce is in his study, breathing deeply over the rough draft of a new story. It is always difficult to read what you have just written, if you have any imagination. He is trying to pretend he is someone else; the publisher's reader, for instance. But instead of reading the words in front of him, he finds himself wondering whether the reader has a moustache. This won't do. He crosses his legs under the table and closes his eyes for a moment. Then he opens them again, clears his throat and begins reading aloud. The tone of his voice interests him. He breaks off for a moment to think. "I wonder whether I would be any good on the wireless?"

Outside it is raining. He is looking out of the window, and suddenly he sees his wife dashing off down the drive. "Where on earth is she going?"

He starts thinking of all the things she might possibly be doing outside at half-past ten on a rainy morning. "Shopping? But she doesn't do the shopping." A picture of vans coming up the drive forms itself in his mind, and a voice, Eileen's voice, says, "That's one good thing about living in the country, one doesn't have to stand in queues, the food is brought." Now, when did she say that?

He can't see his wife any more now, she has gone round a bend in the drive. "What *is* she up to? Nobody pays visits at half-past ten in the morning. Why isn't she upstairs painting? Ah! Perhaps she's off to get someone for this portrait. But I told her not to bring them here! Oh, what a worry. No wonder I can't get on with my work."

It was then that nurse knocked on the study door.

Mr. Noyce put on a very sad expression and said, "Come in," gently.

Nurse knocked again (she hadn't heard him).

"Oh, damn it—come in, can't you?" Mr. Noyce shouted.

"There now, you've made me slop the tea," nurse said, closing the door behind her.

"Tea?" Mr. Noyce said. "Who said I wanted tea early?"

"But it's gone half-past eleven," nurse said, putting down the tea.

Mr. Noyce peered at the clock. "And now my eyesight is going!" he said. "It's one damn thing after another. What with these constant interruptions—how do you suppose I'm ever going to get on with my work?"

Nurse had already moved away towards the door, when he called her back. "One minute," he said. "What's my wife doing out in the rain like that?"

"I'm sure I don't know, Master Harry," nurse said.

"You know, that fire has upset my nerves," Mr. Noyce said. "I can't work properly, I don't see straight, I've lost my powers of concentration. I keep on feeling something awful is going to happen."

"Oh, it's that party, that's what it is. You are thinking of the party on Saturday, Master Harry. It is a worry," said nurse. Then she told him about Mrs. Walmby.

Mrs. Walmby was not really a bad-tempered woman, and neither did she nurse her grievances.

Living in the country, shut off, for the most part, from the rest of mankind, there was no one to tell her what a wonderful servant she was, to dangle the prospect of less work and higher wages before her, to tell her she was wasted. And so, as far as anyone can be, she was content.

"Leave it to me, Ma'am," she had always said. Only the most foolish would disobey this command. For it is better to have the sort of things to eat that a cook thinks you ought to like to eat, or on bad days deserve to eat, than to insist on what you want and never get it. "The master says he would love to have an apple-pie" or "The master never really cared for tripe"—such words as these, gently spoken, almost confided, and followed by a sigh would often enough change Mrs. Walmby's mind for her. But to be told straight off—"Clear soup, mayonnaise of salmon, roast chicken, mushrooms on toast followed by dessert," and to be handed the list, made her exclaim at once, "I should never be able to manage—and where, may I ask, is the salmon coming from?" Which is what happened last week, when Mrs. Noyce suddenly realised that the party was inevitable and something had to be done. Ever since then there has been trouble threatening in the kitchen. And Linda going (Mrs. Walmby could not make out just why, though she had her suspicions) and the fire in the airing cupboard—all these things have upset routine, a thing indispensable to life in the kitchen. And Mrs. Walmby is not young; she is very nearly seventy. So when Mr. Noyce comes into the kitchen, brought there by nurse, she rises up from her chair, distant and proud like some abandoned queen, risking no words.

"Now, what's all this trouble?" Mr. Noyce said. And got no answer.

"Nurse tells me you are a bit upset," he said, turning to nurse for confirmation.

"Good morning, Sir," cook said.

"Good morning. Please do sit down."

"I prefer to stand."

What can a man do in such circumstances? He cannot humble himself without appearing to grovel, and to be dignified in the face of a so much greater dignity means playing the difficult game of second-fiddle. But luckily nurse was there.

"The master has interrupted his work to come to speak to you," she said. "He is worried about the party."

Mrs. Walmby raised her eyebrows. "The master is always welcome in my kitchen," she said; "but there is no cause for him to be disturbed."

"Look here, I'm fed up with this party. Let's call the whole thing off," Mr. Noyce said.

"Oh, Sir! We couldn't do that," Mrs. Walmby said.

"Of course we could."

"Not without hurting people's feelings. And at the last moment, like that!" nurse said.

"People's feelings!" cried Mr. Noyce. "What about my feelings! Ham-sandwiches every day of the week for lunch! I like that!"

"But you've only got to say, Sir. Why ever didn't you tell me, now, and I would have made you an omelette or bacon and eggs—anything so long as you are pleased," cook said.

"Well, it's not your fault," Mr. Noyce said. "The whole thing is a fearful mistake."

Mr. Broom came in at the back door just then. He walked across and put a dead rabbit on the drying-board by the sink, and went back and out through the door without saying a word.

"Rather rude, isn't he? What's the matter with him?" Mr. Noyce said.

"It's his wife," nurse said quietly. "He has been getting like that ever since his wife left."

"Enough to make any man happy, not depressed," Mr. Noyce said.

Mrs. Walmby and nurse exchanged a long, horrified look.

"Oh come on, a joke's a joke!" Mr. Noyce said. "Don't stand there looking so gloomy. Tell us what we are going to eat for this ridiculous party, Mrs. Walmby. Somebody did tell me. But it didn't suit with my wine."

Mrs. Walmby opened the table drawer and pulled out Mrs. Noyce's list and handed it to Mr. Noyce with two fingers. He read it. "Oh, nonsense," he said. "We don't want that stuff. Really, you women. Don't think I'm being personal, Cook. But why in the world have a long, melancholy, pretentious meal like that? No. This thing needs organising." He tore up the list.

"Oh, Sir!" said cook.

"It's all right," he said. "I'll face the fireworks."

Mrs. Walmby put her hand up to her mouth.

"That's right, have a good laugh. I feel like laughing myself, I don't know why."

A crooked sort of smirk came over nurse's face, but she said nothing.

"Now supposing we have oysters for a start," Mr. Noyce went on. "Oh yes. I can order them. Nothing is impossible."

"But it's Wednesday, Master Harry," nurse said.

"I don't care if it's the Day of Judgment. Don't interrupt me. Then how about partridges cooked inside pheasants to follow? That would be quite nice. And then an enormous number of mince-pies served with a bowl of brandy butter. How about that? Have you ever cooked a peacock, Mrs. Walmby? Now, that's a fine sight on the table. You keep the feathers—"

But this discourse on imaginative meals was interrupted just then by Mrs. Noyce coming in.

"Oh, there you are," she said. "I couldn't make out where everyone was. What's the matter? You all look terribly guilty."

"Well, we've torn up your meal," Mr. Noyce said. He pointed to the bits on the floor.

"Just as well," Mrs. Noyce said, "because there isn't going to be a dinner party. And that's that."

This gave them all a shock, perhaps because the way she said it sounded so definite. Mr. Noyce recovered first.

"How do you mean?" he said.

Mrs. Noyce walked out of the kitchen. Nurse and Mrs. Walmby looked at the floor, and muttering under his breath, Mr. Noyce followed his wife.

He caught up with her in the hall, saying, "Eileen I What the hell—Eileen, really!"

"Oh, go away," she said.

"No, I want to talk to you."

"You bore me to death. I hate you."

"But, Eileen! Whatever is the matter?"

Mrs. Noyce burst into tears.

"I like Barbara and John," she said. "I could be friends with them. I like the way they live. I like the children and the house and everything, and I hate it here! I hate the emptiness and loneliness. I hate the way you laugh at everything. I'm not going to have people I like laughed at the way you laugh. Oh, I want to get away, go away anywhere, absolutely anywhere as long as it's not here!" She ran upstairs.

"Tantrums. Oh dear, tantrums," said poor Mr. Noyce.

Mrs. Noyce is of course an artist, which should make up for not having children, but even before Nature intended her to be a mother she had been an unstable person. Her own mother had been a sentimental Woman who had insisted upon the girls having as good an education as the boys, with the result that Eileen went to extremely expensive boarding-schools (she was always unhappy, so she kept on leaving, but there was always another), where they tried to teach her to behave like a lady. So at the age of eighteen she was let loose on the world, discontented, quite incapable of earning a living, and quite unable to spell. Both her parents considered she ought to get married, but they failed to take any practical steps in the matter and were very surprised and indignant when she took things into her own hands and married a complete outsider (not Mr. Noyce). This, or something like it, must have happened to thousands of others, the only difference being that Eileen loved painting. Her father had taken it seriously at first, and had encouraged her to look at posters and spoken warmly about commercial art. But by this time Eileen had had enough of schooling and refused to be taught anything further. After her divorce (she left her first husband, being unhappy again), she spent what little money she had in Paris; where she found out a little more about painting, what it is like to be hungry, and how, although life is very difficult, it need not always be nasty. But in the end her education prevailed. Along came Mr. Noyce, and in the twinkling of an eye, there she was—if not exactly the Lady of the Manor—as near to it as you can ever get these days.

"*Must* you behave like a child of twelve?" said Mr. Noyce to his wife that evening. (She was still in a highly emotional state.)

"I don't care any more," she said. "I'm finished, I'm done."

"Ridiculous!" said Mr. Noyce. "Just because one of your pictures has gone wrong! Why, if I made half the fuss you make when I get stuck with my stories, or if poor old Broom with his wife gone—"

"It's got nothing to do with my painting," Mrs. Noyce interrupted him.

"Look here," he said, making himself as comfortable as possible on the sofa, "Look here, Eileen, you are an artist. And one day you are going to be a good one, if only you stick to your work. Maybe I was wrong asking you to take on household responsibilities. Yes, I was wrong. We are both such egoists, that's the root of the trouble. Well, look here, God knows how we are going to afford it, but we'll have a housekeeper here. You can engage one. Now will you pull yourself together? I do so hate it when women cry."

"But I *want* to run my own house! I'm sick of painting—what's the good of it all. I want to have a home and children, and be human."

"Oh, God," Mr. Noyce said.

"I'm young now, still young enough, anyway," Mrs. Noyce went on; "but soon I won't be young any more, and it'll be too late."

"The sooner the better. Who's been telling you you look pretty, Eileen?"

"What's that got to do with it?"

"Everything," he said. "You see, that is why it is so difficult for a woman to be an artist. Whatever a man does, the woman who lives with him thinks herself exploited. Why did you marry me? Because, you said, I believed in you as an artist. Oh yes, you said that. And what happens when I treat you with respect in accordance with the view you have of yourself as an artist? You turn on me and demand a home and children—all the things I have sheltered you from and from which an artist must be delivered. In return, and there must be a give and take, I ask that you should paint. As to what is the good of it all, there just isn't an answer. What is the good of being a mother?"

"I shall never be a great artist," she said.

"My dear, you'd certainly never make a great mother—if there is such a thing. Somehow it makes me think of a cow, I don't know why."

"How hateful of you to make fun of cows!"

"I wasn't. They just occurred to me as archetypal mothers."

"You're going to pay for this," Mrs. Noyce said passionately.

"Well, that's your affair," he said. "If you want to cut off your nose to spite your face—go ahead. But can't we be sensible, Eileen?"

"Oh yes, can't we be friends?" she said, mocking him. "It's always either that, or else 'I can't live without you. We'll make life civilised,' you said. 'You and I understand one another.' Oh yes, I can remember things, too. And look at us! Miserable, bickering, quarrelling strangers cooped up together. That's what we are."

"But you have, after all, been able to get on with your painting—at least until this morning, shall we say?" Mr. Noyce looked down at his hands as though admiring the gold ring on his little finger.

"How you humiliate me!" Mrs. Noyce said.

CHAPTER NINE

"IM WUNDERSCHÖNEN Monat Mai," sang Mr. Noyce quietly, in the bathroom. The oysters were due to arrive any moment now, and Mr. Broom had been so co-operative about the pheasants and partridges that instead of being a worry, the arrangements for the party had been a pleasure to handle. Even if the whole thing had been rather expensive, what after all, does expense matter compared with the fun of succeeding at somebody else's job?

"Well now, bless him! It's done Master Harry good to have his own way," nurse was saying downstairs in the study. It was her privilege to keep this room tidy, and she spoke to herself while doing the dusting. Mr. Noyce never bothered to put his things away, so there were generally a number of books to be put back on the shelves, and when he wrote in his diary, this too was left on the table. Nurse always read the last entry before dusting the covers and putting the book in the drawer. When you have taught a child to write, have enthused over his first trembling pothooks, have later on kept all his letters to you in a little box with butterfly wings on the lid, and later still when the child, grown to a man, has published books that you helped him to write (all of them are on a special shelf with the Bible, where you can reach them easily from your chair by the fireside)—when, in fact, from the word go you have presided over a man's writing, it comes quite natural to read anything written in that well-known hand. And nurse always kept what was private private. Who does keep a diary strictly for himself? Isn't it always addressed to someone, or aimed at a future generation? Somehow or other, I think it is meant to be published. This is what nurse had just read:.

"I do think people like myself have a duty towards society. After all, in the past it was we who entertained, and having learned the art, we are to blame if it dies out. These days there is a fatal lack of gaiety among people of all classes. Nobody has private parties any more, everything is organised from the outside, and such entertainments as there are, are all public. We have forgotten how to amuse ourselves. Even my parents knew how to be gay on occasions, and in every large household in the country there were regular parties at which young people could meet and get to know each other and old trouts in extraordinary habillement could enjoy themselves in their own fashion. And as short a while ago as the twenties, what wonderful parties there were in London! The Byzantine party, for instance, with everyone, including the waiters, in as near as possible Byzantine attire. How handsome it made the women look, I remember. Those rather severe dresses and chandelier jewellery hanging in huge clusters suit tall women, and roast peacock makes a fine sight on the table. The resinous Greek wine was a bit too heavy, but it was a splendid occasion. There is nothing like that to-day. And all to the good perhaps, because it is a sign of decadence when one generation imitates the other. Nowadays, in a material world, amusement is mechanical. Hotels run parties for what is left of the upper classes, and the rest have their 'amusement' parks, 'fun' fairs, football pools, the cinema and the Dogs. I feel it serves them right. 'To each is given what defeat he will.' One learns how true that is as one grows old. I forget who said it, but it is not just a clever remark.

"And so my party is a gesture; not a very lavish one, and not very amusing either, for the middle path is the one I am forced to follow. All middle-aged or older, I and my guests are at that time of life when hope for the future means having the same amount of time to live in forwards as there is backwards. We have become fond of life as never before when we were young and life was a gift; for now, whatever we may have wanted, life has belonged to us so long that it seems we made it."

To read this almost made nurse cry. The tears hung about in her eyes as she dusted. "Bless him, bless him," she repeated. The tears never dropped, they gradually disappeared. "But it's not so hard when you are old," she said to herself; "and the time will come when he puts all that behind him, I know it will. And then he can rest himself and be at peace. He hasn't got Faith, like me. But he's good—he's good all through, I know him. And if I know, then the Lord knows, too. Bless him! But bless me—I've got a lot of work to do to-day!"

Later on that morning nurse had to visit Mrs. Noyce in her studio.

"I don't know what it is," Mrs. Noyce said as she came in, "but it does seem to me that a party creates a disturbing atmosphere in the house. I do hope it's not like this afterwards, as well as before. I can't get any work done this morning."

"Well, I'm sorry I'm sure," nurse said; "but I haven't climbed all those stairs just for nothing, Miss Eileen."

"I didn't mean it was you. Why do you always take what I say so personally? Is something the matter, Nurse—I suppose you want me to come down?"

"Mrs. Darlington has called and wants to see you," nurse said.

Downstairs Mrs. Darlington was hugging her elbows in the servants' hall.

"Who ever put you in here," Mrs. Noyce said, coming in with a rush, still carrying her palette and looking as though she meant to be off again the next minute. Nurse followed, quietly closing the door from outside.

"I'm ever so sorry to disturb you on a day like this when you must be so busy," Mrs. Darlington said. She looked curiously at the palette. This made Mrs. Noyce feel self-conscious.

"It's paint," she said. "I paint, you know."

"Yes, we did hear you did."

"This is where the paint goes before you put it on the canvas."

"There now."

"Yes, it's quite a job painting a picture, though you might not think so."

"Oh, it is, I'm sure! It must be ever so difficult keeping to all those colours."

"Yes," said Mrs. Noyce.

There was a silence, and then both of them spoke together and neither heard what the other one said.

"You want to tell me something, don't you?" Mrs. Noyce said after a moment. "I'm so sorry, I'm always in a bit of a daze after painting. It's so stupid of them to have put you in here. Let's go somewhere where it's warm."

"Oh no, Ma'am!" Mrs. Darlington said, letting go her elbows. "If you don't mind, I would rather speak to you here. It's about Linda I've come, as you might guess.

Nobody likes to feel ashamed of their own daughter, but we do feel ashamed, Ma'am. Mr. Darlington feels so ashamed that he couldn't come, so I had to come. But so as I can look you in the face, I'd like you to know, Ma'am, that I'm ready and willing to put myself in my daughter's place and come up and give a hand if I'm needed to-night. Linda's told us the truth. I don't know whatever made her tell such lies, I'm sure. I never was so ashamed in all my life. And the worst is, that I did believe it."

Her head drooped and her face screwed up. She wept in pain.

"Oh, now don't do that!" Mrs. Noyce said. She put her palette down on the red tablecloth that covered the disused servants' dining-table. Dust rose up. "Oh dear, can't we forget all about it? It was always so silly, and it's like a bad dream coming now."

"I don't know what you must think of us," Mrs. Darlington said.

Mrs. Noyce shivered.

"It's not your fault," she said. "She must be a very unhappy girl, Linda, behaving like that. It's very queer when you come to think of it, isn't it? I wonder if there is anything one could do. Because she can't be normal."

"Oh, she's had her punishment, Ma'am."

"Do you think one learns from punishment?"

"If it's hard enough you do. Mr. Darlington isn't a one for the strap, but if it's the strap it's got to be, he knows how to use it."

"The strap?"

"Yes. Some do call it a bit old-fashioned. But if you want them to grow up straight, they've got to be hurt, I say. What's the good of a tap on the hands? They're not going to remember that. Punishment's got to be punishment."

"You mean, you beat her?"

"Yes, Ma'am; what she did needed the strap."

"But how *wicked*—no wonder the girl is mad!" Mrs. Darlington straightened herself. "No, Ma'am; I'll not have you say that. My girl is all right. It doesn't follow that when she does wrong she is queer. And she's taken her punishment."

"I can't bear this," said Mrs. Noyce. "Let me speak to Linda. Send her up here."

"Oh no, Ma'am; that wouldn't be seemly at all."

"Do you think I care? Oh, how stupid everyone is! Then I'll go back with you this minute, Mrs. Darlington."

Mr. Noyce was just taking some bottles of wine into the dining-room where nurse had lit the fire, when his wife came into the hall, dashed past him and began to put her coat on.

"Where on earth are you off to now?" he said.

"To the Darlington's," Mrs. Noyce said. "They beat Linda. I'm not going to have it."

"Just a minute," he said. "Here, come in here."

He went into the dining-room and put the bottles down on the table. She stood by the door, trying to get her arm into the armhole of her coat. He took hold of her free hand and marched her towards the fire.

"Fool," he said. "Do you know what you're doing? Making a laughing-stock of yourself. And me. Now what is this all about? This is not the way to prepare for a party. Do you want to have us all upset?"

"It's a cruel and wicked thing to beat children," Mrs. Noyce said.

"Of course it is. But what can you do about it?"

"Speak to her."

"Poor little creature. What good is that going to do?"

"Show her we don't approve, that we wouldn't have done it."

"Eileen, did I make any fuss over this business? Have you ever thought about it from my point of view? Didn't I always say, leave the damn thing alone, it'll die down. And now you want to fan up the flames and make trouble. It's too bad of you."

"If only you would stop talking, I might explain," Mrs. Noyce said. Then she told him about Mrs. Darlington's visit and what she had said.

"You know," he said afterwards, "I am quite sure that the best thing to do in the circumstances is to do as I always said. Let things be. But I can't convince you, and I don't want to have a row. So I am going to talk to Mrs. Darlington myself. You know how hopeless you are, Eileen, with anything like this. All over the place. Well, I'm not so emotional. I'm going to suggest to Mrs. Darlington that we let bygones be bygones. And to show I really mean this, I'm going to suggest both Linda and her mother come up to help for the party. That will put an end to gossip and give the girl a chance to get back her dignity. Yes. I shall do that. You can't say I'm not taking trouble over my party."

"Oh, all right," Mrs. Noyce said wearily. "It's obvious I'm not going to get any painting done to-day. You do as you like."

Meanwhile a ghastly mixture of bad temper and burnt pastry prevailed over everything else in the kitchen atmosphere. "Never again," Mrs. Walmby said, tackling that enormous number of mince-pies.

Mrs. Ethelburger's Irene hung about, doing neither one thing nor the other, but polishing the silver a bit, greasing a few pastry tins now and then, and looking with astonishment at the mound of butter and sugar nurse was trying to dominate.

"Brandy butter. Get on with your work," nurse said.

"Sluts. That's what they are nowadays. Don't know what work is," Mrs. Walmby said. "Come here, girl. You can open the oven door for me."

"We have electricity," Irene said.

"I daresay," said Mrs. Walmby; "but you don't have any parties."

"Ooh! We do! You should see us at Christmas and—"

"Now it's no good contradicting, because nobody's listening. See?" Mrs. Walmby knelt down and put another batch of pies into the oven.

"Do you want any more coal brought in?" Mr. Broom said, putting his head round the door. "I've trimmed the birds up for you, and if there's nothing else for me to do, I'll be off."

"Here, just you stop making draughts in my kitchen!" Mrs. Walmby said. "What do you think my pastry is going to be like if you keep on opening that door with my oven open?"

Mr. Broom withdrew, and slammed the door behind him.

"Just like a man to make a nuisance of himself when he's wanted. Who's going to get my coal in now, I should like to know! Oh, whatever am I going to do; I shall go balmy."

"Never mind," nurse said. "It's better with him out of the way. He's getting more and more queer tempered. And men do so get in the way."

"Mrs. Ethelburger says it's men make the cookers all wrong because they like to think of a woman on her knees when she puts things in the oven and breaking her back over the sink because it's too low. Oh, she's got ever such funny things to say she has. Sometimes I just can't help laughing!" Irene began to giggle.

"Well, there's nothing to laugh at now," Mrs. Walmby said.

"Oh dear! Is something burning? What can I do to help?" Mrs. Noyce said, coming into the kitchen.

"We shall manage," Mrs. Walmby said. She began rolling out pastry with vigour.

Mr. Spark wandered about his garden. There was a sad and not very humorous smile on his face and the cold made his eyes water. His large, shadowy garden was a cold place that morning. The grass curled under a load of rime, and where the sun touched them the trees dripped, and everywhere leaves fell continually after the first real frost of the year. The Rector carried a basket filled with little green tomatoes, which now would never ripen. He had been warned not to leave them out in the frost, but having planted them late in the year, few had ripened, and day by day while the weather remained so lovely, he had promised himself, "To-morrow I shall bring them in, I shall leave them just this one more day." And the frost had struck.

"Next year I shall remember," he said.

He saw Mrs. White coming out of the house towards him, and quickened his pace.

"Well, no wonder I couldn't find you," Mrs. White said. Drips hung from the end of her nose, and her breath showed in puffs like gentle steam. "Never thought you'd be out this weather. There's tea for you in the kitchen."

They walked back to the house together.

"And now it is winter, as quickly as that," Mr. Spark said. "It is like waking up. I have dreamed away the summer."

"But it is a natural thing," Mrs. White said. "It makes a change, the way things follow. I like winter myself. It is a time of rest, after all that summer. You couldn't go on making jam and bottling the fruit for ever."

"No. Everything needs rest. You have never wanted to live in a hot climate, have you, Mrs. White?"

"I've never thought. If you had nothing to do like in the Garden of Eden, it might be all right. But we can't go back there, so I'd rather be here."

They reached the house and went in.

Mrs. Spark was waiting for them in the kitchen.

"Whatever have you got there?" she said to her husband. "I hope I'm not supposed to deal with the miserable things. Here's your tea. You haven't forgotten it's the party to-night, have you?"

"Mrs. White and I were talking about the Garden of Eden," Mr. Spark said.

"Really?" Mrs. Spark said, pouring out another cup. "Here's yours, Mrs. White, and afterwards, would you mind giving my shoes a good polish? I've put them out by my bed."

"Thank you. Yes, I will. It must have been queer in that garden, if you come to think of it," Mrs. White said.

"Queer?" said Mrs. Spark. "Well, it's a queer world altogether, really; isn't it? We mustn't be too long over tea this morning, there's a great deal of work to be done."

"But fancy being all alone with no work and no children, and one man and God and the Devil. Queer to find yourself with all that time on your hands, and the days of the week slipping by and nothing to do. And no one of her own sort to talk to, that must have come hard on the woman."

"It's only a story," Mrs. Spark said, "and, anyway, before the Fall they were all happy. That's the point, don't you think. We don't realise what happiness is until it's been taken away."

"And suppose it wasn't her fault, things wouldn't have been any different. Somebody had to pick the apple, otherwise why was it there? There's always some purpose. And it's right it was her because if he'd done it she'd have still had to suffer, and it wouldn't be fair." Mrs. White drank up her tea.

"But you women, you don't seem to have any poetry in your souls!" Mr. Spark said.

"Oh now, come on," said Mrs. Spark. "Eleven o'clock in the morning is no time for poetry—we've got work to do!"

"But it's always time for poetry. The reason life is so hard and so dull is because we never stop to praise God and give Him thanks for His creation. That is poetry."

"Yes. Well, now, couldn't you use that for your sermon to-morrow? You could be jotting it down while we get on," Mrs. Spark said.

Once more the Rector is in his garden; not alone this time, but with Mr. Browning, who has called with a spray of carnations from his hothouse for Mrs. Spark to wear at the party. They stand leaning over the gate watching the river water flow past at the end of the garden. The sun has dispersed the morning mist and melted the frost, and the few clouds in the sky are so high up that they seem thousands of miles away.

"This is where we come and rest ourselves in summer at the end of the day," the Rector said.

"Does your wife ever rest? I can't imagine it," Mr. Browning said.

"She is rather a fiend for work. Don't you think most women are?" said the Rector.

"They like us depending on them, otherwise how can they feel important?" Mr. Browning said. "Look at my old mother, still toiling away. And what would she do if she hadn't got me to look after? Of course, I am grateful! But sometimes I feel, if you can understand, it's a bit of a nuisance this everlasting being looked after. I mean, what they don't see, or don't want to see, is one *can* stand on one's own feet. It's a problem."

"Yes, it's a very powerful emotion, the love of a woman for her children. My wife has never got over our tragedy. And there is nothing that I can do to repair that loss, except to blame myself for being inadequate. It is sad for us both," the Rector said.

"There's religion," Mr. Browning said.

"Oh, I don't think religion means much to a woman," Mr. Spark said. "It's not the same for a woman as for a man. Not that a woman can't be devout, we know that from the Saints. But with the usual lot, like those of my congregation, and there are many more women than men in my congregation, religion is like some sort of jewellery that they put on, an extravagance given to them by men which among themselves they think of, possibly, as rather beautiful but certainly unnecessary. And I love them for it, as one must. I have a deep feeling of compassion for women. We may know that to have the power and the glory means nothing—vanity, all is vanity—but to women who have never had these things, or achieved them rarely by some fault or sport of reasoning in the affairs of men, power and glory are the highest aims, the cruellest dreams. I know things change, and it is a very different world to-day from the world my mother lived in. They tell me women rule America. Perhaps they do. And people say, 'Women are men's equals now.' But they are not. Because they have confused equality with imitation. They ape us. We should be flattered. I am going to say a rather daring thing. I don't think women have souls. Or if they have, they are not the same kind as ours. That comes strangely from a clergyman! But I deal with souls, they are my concern. And never once in all my days have I known a woman with something to offer to God. Not even her sorrow or her pain, for they are hers and she will not give them up. But with what humility and grace a woman takes! Read about them in the Bible, and thinking only of the best, of Mary, one is ashamed."

It seemed Mr. Browning had nothing to say on the subject. His face looked sad. He watched the river flowing by, and sighed.

"I'm sorry I talked like that," the Rector said. "Forgive me. But it's not often I have an intelligent audience. And besides, I feel you are an old friend, you understand?"

Still watching the river, and in that tone of voice one uses sometimes to describe a dream, "Do you know the legend of Faust?" Mr. Browning said. "I read it as a boy. The story of a man with ambition who was damned. And there is another version which I read much later on where Faust is saved. In both there is a lot about the love of women, but it never seemed to me that mattered one way or the other; Faust would be Faust. And I, being Faust— not so much now, no, goodness knows I am a nobody now in my imagination—I, being Faust, knew that there were powers outside me against which I had to be tested. I didn't think of success or failure, the struggle itself was great enough for me. But Faust in the story, it seems, was an old man, well, middle-aged as I am now, and it was too early to be Faust as a boy. I hadn't understood. You know, I was not educated. And I am still, outside my own job, an ignorant person. You called me intelligent. Well, all that means is that compared to the youth I was, the man I have become is without dignity. 'Old friend,' you said; well, old friend, I am one of the women in your congregation. You see, I haven't a soul because I don't feel any more there is anything powerful outside me. That's about it."

"It's strange—" the Rector began, but was violently interrupted. The two had become so engrossed in themselves and each other that they had never noticed Mrs. White come bearing down on them from the house.

"I'm sorry to disturb you two gentlemen," she suddenly called out behind them; "but it's gone half-past, and the Missus says if he wants to stay to lunch Mr. Browning is very welcome. But would you please come in now."

"Oh dear—what an awful shock you gave me!" the Rector said. "Really, you should be careful. I can feel my heart!"

Mrs. White looked down her nose. "I'm ever so sorry," she said. "I called, didn't you hear me? But you've kept your lunch waiting more than half an hour."

Mrs. Flint and Mr. Ethelburger sat before the fire. The children were resting, and Mrs. Ethelburger was having a rest that day because of the party. It was a peaceful hour.

"I hope Barbara will wear a nice dress this evening," Mrs. Flint said, "she must look her best."

"She always looks nice to me," Mr. Ethelburger said.

Mrs. Flint edged herself forward in her chair. "I don't know whether you've noticed," she said, "but Barbara has been looking awfully tired lately."

Mr. Ethelburger looked at his mother-in-law sideways, good-humouredly and with the happy degree of tolerance that the strong show for the weak. "You ought to have had a son," he said, "then you *would* have had something to worry about."

"I never wanted a son," Mrs. Flint said shortly. "I thought every woman wanted a son."

"Well, that's your mistake."

"Oh now, come, Mother, you know I was teasing!"

"Dear John. And you are so very kind to me. It's not easy, I know, having to live with a mother-in-law."

"But it's not much fun for you," Mr. Ethelburger said.

"It's all I ask. You know how I love my daughter."

"Far, far too much!"

"You are laughing at me. But I'd rather you did. It's the right way to treat a penniless, doting old woman like myself! I know I'm silly. Once I was proud, but it doesn't do to be too stiff-necked if you're going to go on and endure." A gentle half-hidden look of joy undid the harmed expression that was usual on her face. "And I have my reward," she said. "You see, when I was young I was pretty. Not lovely, like Barbara is, but the sort that was fashionable then. Elegant you might call it, but it was the way men liked women to be then. And of course I was courted, and as you know, I chose the wrong one. He married me for my money. But even when I knew, and he made it quite clear, oh, quite clear from the beginning, I went on loving him then. Odd, isn't it? And how he hated me for it! That's the funny thing about men, they don't want love or anything absolute. No, you need not contradict me, you can't understand my point of view, one couldn't expect you to— you know I'm silly! But a mother's love is a real love, and Barbara is my reward."

"And so you think I don't love Barbara enough," Mr. Ethelburger said. "Now, you know, that is rather impertinent of you."

"I didn't mean that, not at all!" Mrs. Flint said, laughing.

"You want me to 'Love her for herself alone and not her yellow hair,' then. But that's impossible."

"Men always quote poetry when they want to muddle a woman, and I never could see any connection between real love and poetry. But you'll get cross if I go on, and we can't have that."

"Well, you just stop worrying yourself about Barbara and me," said Mr. Ethelburger, "and then all three of us will be happy. Now I must get on with my work. All this sitting about in the afternoon talking doesn't do a man any good."

The dogs followed him out of the room. Mrs. Flint got up and closed the door, which, as usual, was left open behind the procession. Coming back to the fireside, she settled herself down in her chair comfortably.

"I suppose it's all right really," she said. "But perhaps it's as well he isn't very intelligent." She closed her eyes for a bit, and began to doze.

CHAPTER TEN

"WELL, thanks, Broom, for helping to-day," Mr. Noyce said. "It's good of you to work in the house like that. Thank you."

"You're welcome," Mr. Broom said. "I'll be off, then. Good night."

"Good night."

It was between times, neither day nor night. The sun had gone, leaving behind a slowly ebbing light; the sky looked quiet and undisturbed, and among the dark trees it was quiet. Mr. Noyce, standing on the steps outside the front door of his house, watched Mr. Broom down the drive till he could see him no more. Lights went on in the house. White smoke poured out of one of the chimneys. Someone began shutting windows, and the excited voices of women calling each other sounded from inside the house. And then the curtains were drawn. A large bird slid out from the trees without noise and without shadow, and a long, thin cat came swiftly over the grass as though drawn on wheels. Two fluttering lights appeared in the distance down the drive, and faintly voices could be heard. The lights grew and the subdued voices conversed.

"Lonely down here."

"What time's the company expected?"

"Dinner's at eight, I keep on telling you."

"Don't shout. You've got to behave yourself."

"There you go—making me feel nervous."

"Now you help in the kitchen, as I said. I'll do the waiting at table."

"Here, Mum! This way. You don't want to go in at the front."

It was Linda and her mother on bicycles coming to help for the party. The lights vanished, and their voices drifted away as they circled round to the back.

"Puss, puss, puss!" nurse suddenly called from a downstairs window. "Puss, puss, puss—you are a naughty cat! Well, if you get run over now, you've brought it on yourself."

"Oh, shut up," Mr. Noyce said under his breath. He waited just a moment or two longer, and then went in.

It was a whole two hours before the beginning of the party. "Too soon to change," Mr. Noyce said, looking at his watch. He opened the dining-room door, but did not go in. The table was laid with a white cloth and brightly shining cutlery and silver. Firelight leapt in the prisms of cut-glass, and there was no other light than the fire. Boiling sap and hissing flames and the visible pulse of the flames lighting the walls conjured out of the warm emptiness and fire noises a mysterious, gay life. Mr. Noyce withdrew his head and shut the door. He looked at his watch again. "A glass of sherry," he said to himself.

He found his wife in the drawing-room, doing her nails.

"Sorry," she said, "but it's so much warmer down here than upstairs."

"Heavens!" Mr. Noyce said. "Tell them to light a fire in your bedroom. Let's have some sherry." Stretching a finger out, he leaned on the bell.

"The party has gone to your head," Mrs. Noyce said. She went on with her nails.

"Put on lots of jewellery," Mr. Noyce said. "Don't, for God's sake, worry about good taste. Wear that stuff of Mother's. And do make up your face. And wear a whole lot of rings, not just that engagement thing. You're good looking, Eileen; you want to take trouble over yourself."

"Thank you," Mrs. Noyce said.

Nurse came in just then. "Did you ring?" she said. She came over to the fire and fixed her master with a grave and rather baffling look which generally heralded a moral lecture; in any case, it was not the expression of a servant about to take an order.

"Sherry," Mr. Noyce said.

"It's very thoughtless of you, Master Harry, to start ringing bells just now. And isn't it time you changed?" nurse said.

Mr. Noyce leaned over the back of his chair and touched the bell again. "When I say sherry, I mean sherry," he said. "If you won't, then someone else will have to take my orders."

Nurse did not flinch. As though dealing with a most usual situation, she bowed her head, murmuring "Very well, Master Harry," and walked out, not angry but sorry.

"And take a week's notice if you like," Mr. Noyce called after her.

The door closed.

"Honestly, Harry, you are childish," Mrs. Noyce said. She held her hand out and examined her nails.

"That's what comes of living with a lot of silly women," Mr. Noyce said. "Now, do stop having the sulks, Eileen. I do what I can for you. And I've put a hell of a lot of work into this party."

Mrs. Noyce turned round from the fire. "Do you think I'm going to enjoy talking rubbish to the fatuous village people you've invited? Do you think I want to do that?" she said.

"I seem to remember it was you suggested it in the first place," Mr. Noyce said. "But never mind. What do you want, then? Imagine that I am someone extraordinary—a witch or a magician. There now—what can I do for you, what do you *really* want, Eileen?"

"I should like a powerful car to drive me away."

"Where to?"

"The ends of the earth. Anywhere a long way away."

"But you'd still be you wherever you were."

"How do you know? You wouldn't be there to torment me."

"You would immediately re-create me. It's no good, Eileen, you can't run away from yourself. These clichés are horribly true, you know. Just listen a moment and don't interrupt me. I have been feeling different and more different all day. That's a wonderful thing to feel when you're as old as me. I have turned again! So let me be childish and foolish and gay—that's all on the surface. Underneath, I am consoled. Yes, I really do feel it. I woke up this morning like that, and instead of the feeling fading away at the first touch of reality, everything that happens grows me the way I want to grow. And now I've made up my mind. It was Broom really, being so decent. He *cares* about this place. He may not like you or me, but he knows where he belongs. And I thought as I watched him go off this evening—it's a queer thing this feeling of place, why not let it get hold of one, and stop thinking one might get away? Because I belong here more than to most places. So we are not going to cut our losses and sell the house and drift away. And if you say you can't paint here, all that means is, you can't paint anywhere. And I shall write my ridiculous stories and live on capital, and end up with my ancestors in the graveyard. Which reminds me, we *must* do something about father's grave. The weeds have become a disgrace."

"What an extraordinary thing to think about before a party!" Mrs. Noyce laughed.

But Mr. Noyce continued to be solemn. "At bottom, you are a frivolous-minded person," he said. "With half your gifts I would have made something of myself. But you don't believe in yourself or anybody else. If you were a man, I'd say stop snivelling and get on with it."

Nurse came in with the sherry.

"Come on!" Mr. Noyce said. "You women look like a couple of death's-heads. Let's all have a drink, and then get on with the party."

"Perhaps you have forgotten, Sir, but I am under notice," nurse said.

"Oh dear, how serious everyone is to-night! I withdraw that notice. I eat my words. I am very sorry. But Miss Eileen will bear me out—I *am* master in this house. Now will you have a drink with me?"

"Well I, for one, will not," Mrs. Noyce said. "Somebody's got to take the responsibility, and I think it's time we changed, considering there are guests coming to-night."

There was a pause while she picked up her things and dusted her skirts. And then she went out.

"Exit, chased by a bear," Mr. Noyce said.

"You know, Master Harry, you really must put a brake on your tongue," nurse said. But she accepted a small glass of sherry.

*

A quarter-past seven. The clock had just chimed in the kitchen.

"All right! All right!" Mrs. Walmby said to the clock. She was having a difficult time. Some people have a natural dislike of idleness in others. Cook was one of these; there were so many people hanging about in her kitchen doing nothing, and her power of inventing something to do being exhausted, she just turned her back on them all and spoke to the clock, which could be heard ticking.

"Come on, come on!" she said. "And it's not the first time either I've caught you running slow. All that fuss when most likely it's gone twenty-five past or later! But you don't catch me with your chimes. Oh no. Now, that's enough of you. Five minutes more, and I'll have to look at the ovens. Look smart!" she said, suddenly turning round.

"What's that? Was it the bell ringing?" Mrs. Darlington said.

"No. But it soon will be," said Mrs. Walmby. "Oh dear—I feel queer—it's all this standing. Can't I sit down a bit?" said Irene.

"Out!" Mrs. Walmby said. "Out of my kitchen! Do you think I haven't got enough to worry about without you feeling queer?"

The bell rang. Everyone looked up. The little shutter over the space marked "Front Door" quivered frantically.

"There now—they've started!" cried Mrs. Walmby. "It's beginning at last."

Outside the front door the Rector was peering at his watch. But the moon wasn't bright enough, and so he couldn't see what time it was.

"Do you know, I think we're a bit early?" he said.

"Oh, surely not. I do so hate being first," Mrs. Spark said. "What on earth shall we talk about? Do you think they are ever going to answer the door?"

"It *was* to-night, dear, wasn't it?"

"Of course it was."

"Perhaps I didn't push hard enough."

"No, no, Arthur; someone's coming."

Mrs. Darlington, in a white apron and with a white cap on her head, opened the front door. She knew how to do the thing properly. "Good evening," she said, smiling. "Please will you come in. This way for your coat and hat, Sir. And if you will follow me, I will show you the way upstairs, Madam."

"Oh dear, I'm afraid we're early," Mrs. Spark said, taking in the tidy room with no coats thrown over the bed.

"Oh no, you're very punctual. Shall I show you the way to the drawing-room when you're ready? You will find Mrs. Noyce waiting downstairs."

All alone with the Rector and his wife for ten minutes, Mrs. Noyce had a hard time of it. Why is it women when they get together at a party so often talk about the sink and the cooker and moths in the cupboard when at home they complain it is just these very things from which they can never get away? In this instance the conversation remained at a thoroughly elementary level, Mrs. Noyce being an ignoramus about the house and Mrs. Spark refusing to talk about anything else, so that in the end the Rector found himself obliged to answer yes, no and good gracious in the right places to build up his wife's stories, just as he did at home. He did this patiently and correctly, sipping from his glass of sherry. But the women looked rather distracted. Mr. Noyce noticed this at once as he came in, beaming and apologising and smelling faintly of attar of roses.

"I expect you are remembering all the occasions you came here when my parents had parties," he said, after the little commotion caused by his entrance had died down. "I do hope now that you are going to find my sort of party as amusing as theirs."

Mr. Browning and his mother came in just then.

"How very nice of you to come," Mr. Noyce said to Mrs. Browning. Everyone noticed at once what a beautiful necklace she was wearing. It was a carved jade pendant hanging from ropes of seed pearls.

"I gave it to her for her birthday," Mr. Browning told everyone with pleasure when Mr. Noyce expressed his admiration.

"What a pity not to hang a thing like that round a young woman's neck," Mr. Noyce murmured to his wife as he poured out the sherry. "You look fine yourself. A little bit more icy and you'd do for the Queen of the Wilis." He set off among his guests with the decanter.

When Mr. and Mrs. Ethelburger arrived, the first and most awkward stage of the party was over. The sherry was beginning to work and the guests talked happily and rather loudly to each other, not being able to hear very clearly what the other one said.

"And how are all your children?" Mrs. Spark enquired, still wearing the smile that had helped so much to describe to Mr. Browning her attitude towards the Rector's gardening.

"Oh, they are very well, thank you," Mrs. Ethelburger said. Her eyes wandered.

"And dear little Chris?" Mrs. Spark insisted, still smiling.

"Oh, he's a bit of a bore really," Mrs. Ethelburger said. ("Thank you, no sherry," she said to Mr. Noyce. "But I insist," he said. "But I don't like sherry.") Yes, Christopher is a difficult child. I suppose he picked it up somewhere in the village, but he goes about singing, 'I wish I were a fascinating bitch and not an illegitimate child'—which isn't what one wants to hear from one's eldest son."

The smile dropped off Mrs. Spark's face at last. Mr. Browning, who had watched Mrs. Ethelburger when she wasn't looking, lit a cigarette, making a to-do about the matches. But Mr. Noyce winked in such a charming way that Mrs. Ethelburger stopped being bad-tempered.

"Children will be children," she said. Which cheered Mrs. Spark enough for her to be able to change the subject in a reasonable way.

"I don't think you've had a chance to speak to my wife yet, have you?" Mr. Noyce said, guiding Mrs. Ethelburger by the elbow. "Here she is. Not enjoying herself a bit, as usual. Eileen, Mrs. Ethelburger is in a frightfully bad temper, and won't drink sherry and uses bad language when talking to Mrs. Spark. Don't you think you and she would get on rather well together?"

Unpardonably Mrs. Noyce had allowed her thoughts to slip away, so that when she looked up suddenly into Mrs. Ethelburger's face, she looked up from the depths of some-where or other—off guard and unfocused on anything really there.

That look startled Mrs. Ethelburger. She said the first thing that came into her head. "Oh! What a shame," she said. "You don't like parties!"

"My dear, if you want to go on dropping bricks you mustn't speak so loud," Mr. Noyce said. Both women blushed.

"How extraordinary you women are," he went on, observing this, "shy, delicately walking creatures—"

"I say, Mr. Noyce," said Mr. Browning, "this is excellent sherry you've got. Sorry, did I interrupt?"

"Not at all. Thank you. Perhaps you'll entertain the ladies while I fill the glasses up," Mr. Noyce said.

Mr. Browning edged himself into a position next to Mrs. Ethelburger. The room was not small, but the company clung together in a small space by the fire, although it was extremely hot.

"Drink up, Eileen!" Mr. Noyce called out, and in that moment Mr. Browning leant forward with an open cigarette-case and said, "Barbara, I must speak to you."

"No, thank you, I'm not smoking," Mrs. Ethelburger said. She looked round for a chair and sat down so that intimate conversation was impossible because there was no other empty chair anywhere near.

"Did you notice the smell of polish when we came in? They seem to have really put themselves out for this party," Mrs. Spark said to her husband, to whom she returned relentlessly although several times they had been parted.

"Well now, you enjoy the occasion," he said.

"Chicken for dinner, I expect," she said, "though I doubt whether Mrs. Noyce cooked it. No, of course, they run to a cook here. She's a very undomesticated lady, Mrs. Noyce."

"Come along! Wives shouldn't talk to husbands at parties, you know," Mr. Noyce said, almost making her jump.

Neither Mr. Ethelburger nor Mrs. Browning were good mixers, but having found each other, they talked quietly and seriously together side by side in two chairs on the fringe of the group by the fire. Mr. Noyce upset all this by bringing up Mrs. Spark. Mr. Ethelburger at once offered her his chair, and then found himself standing face to face with Mr. Noyce.

"Not much fun for you, these parties, I shouldn't think," Mr. Noyce said; "though I don't know why a handsome upstanding young man like yourself shouldn't enjoy himself wherever he is."

As Mr. Ethelburger was handsome, and indeed taller than his host, this sort of remark had as little power to draw him as a reference to the weather. "It's always good to meet one's neighbours," he said. "I don't like my wife getting lonely."

"She's a very beautiful woman, your wife," Mr. Noyce said.

"Yes, she is," said Mr. Ethelburger.

Somehow there seemed nothing more to add, so Mr. Noyce smiled and drifted off. Mrs. Spark and Mrs. Browning were talking about carpets. Mr. Ethelburger drank his sherry and communed with himself. Suddenly there was a total lapse in the conversation, everybody stopped talking at exactly the same moment. Mr. Noyce, who was badgering Mrs. Ethelburger again to have some sherry, closed his eyes and whispered, "Now, who's going to say it?"

"It's not twenty-past, is it?" Mrs. Spark said. "Otherwise of course there's an angel passing over us!"

"Ha, ha, ha," everybody laughed.

"Why do they laugh?" Mr. Noyce said, bending himself a little to be more on a level with Mrs. Ethelburger. "Creatures of habit, aren't they? Well, thank God, that's over. Now, please, do have some sherry. Or let me get you something else. But don't spoil your palate with gin because there is good wine to follow."

"Dinner is served," Mrs. Darlington said, coming in that moment.

The unsubtle and often fatuous chatter was stilled in an instant, although it had only just then reasserted itself. The faces of the guests took on a solemn look. The men coughed, the women patted their hair and looked down at their jewellery. Mrs. Noyce sighed with relief, and Mr.

Noyce made himself important arranging couples and the delicate matter of precedence. He was good at this.

The oysters were a huge success. The wine and the candles and the firelight also had an effect. Do people taste what they eat at parties? "Think what you've got in your mouth," my mother used to say when she had prepared something special and we talked too much. But it is considered rather rude, in England at any rate, if people consume their food in silence at a party. The pheasants stuffed with partridges caused surprise. It proved rather difficult to carve them, but a real conversational hubbub filled the gap while Mr. Noyce achieved it. And after Mr. Noyce's claret had gone the rounds, dissolving the toughness of their hearts, a babbling fantastic friendship closed the gap between neighbours. How pleasant it is to be in this state! The human stomach is a wonderful piece of apparatus, when one comes to think of it. Mr. and Mrs. Spark, who never had dinner (she more than he habitually starving herself), ate hugely without any apparent discomfort. Mrs. Browning, who never touched wine, at first sipped the claret and then drank it with relish.

"Actually, to tell you the truth," Mr. Browning confided in a rather loud voice to Mrs. Noyce, "I don't know anything about this stuff." He held up his glass. "Whisky is my drink. I can tell a good whisky."

"I don't know anything about wine either, but I think it's nice," Mrs. Noyce said.

"It's certainly the making of a good dinner," Mr. Ethelburger said.

"Actually this *tastes* so nice," said Mrs. Spark.

"It reminds me of my youth," the Rector said, "when I was an undergraduate. In those days—"

"But your glass is almost empty!" cried Mr. Noyce. "Here, let me give you some more. Now you drink that."

The Rector did. With a flushed face Mrs. Spark delved into her own history. But even talk of banquets could not sober the company. "My grandfather—" Mrs. Ethelburger began long before the story was finished. They went on talking together.

"Those were the days," Mr. Noyce said to nobody in particular.

"Yes, they were, even for me," said Mrs. Browning, "I'd go back any day, I would."

"Well, I wouldn't," Mr. Browning said, raising his voice, "Give me to-day!" He raised his glass.

"That's right!" Mrs. Noyce said. "One can't go back. And I'm glad." Her face was flushed.

"And of course Emm—that's my sister," Mrs. Spark was telling Mr. Ethelburger, "Emm said—"

(He was silently watching his wife.)

"But my grandfather was a great person, if you know what I mean," Mrs. Ethelburger was saying, holding her glass aslant.

"Drink it, don't play with it," Mr. Browning said.

"And Emm said—"

"M? What does she mean? I love my love with an M because she's moody." But Mrs. Ethelburger, in the presence of her grandfather to all intents and purposes, paid absolutely no attention to anything Mr. Browning had to say. He kicked her under the table.

"Well, what do *you* think?" Mrs. Noyce suddenly asked him.

"Ah, he's a man of many parts, Mr. Browning," the Rector said.

"What? What?" said Mr. Browning. "I'm so sorry, I couldn't have been listening."

"Wine and women, my friend, we were discussing the tastes of women for wine," the Rector said.

"I know nothing about either," said Mr. Browning.

"Oh, surely, surely!"

"No, my dear Mrs. Noyce, I'm a damned ignorant person."

"But that's nice! So nice to be with a person who doesn't know everything."

"Don't you believe him!" the Rector said.

"What are you talking about down there?" Mr. Noyce called out. "Mr. Browning, a drop more claret, and then we'll go on to the next."

"The *next*," Mrs. Browning said. "But he's had quite enough already, I'm sure."

"*In vino veritas*—you'll see," the Rector said to Mrs. Noyce.

"Now, don't start speaking Latin, Arthur, you know what that means," Mrs. Spark said, leaning over the table.

"The women are getting difficult. What hard heads they've got. Is my wife still sober? I do hope not." Mr. Noyce made a sign to Mrs. Darlington, who stood at attention by the sideboard.

"Queer to say that about one's wife, don't you think?" Mrs. Spark murmured in an undertone to Mr. Ethelburger.

"Oh, I don't think he's serious. Besides, nobody's drunk yet," he said.

"Good gracious! I should hope not. Of course, we are not used to all this wine. Tell me, it isn't very strong, really, is it?"

"Well, it's not water. As a matter of fact, it's very good stuff indeed. I shouldn't bother. Just enjoy it."

"I was thinking of Arthur—"

"Oh, don't worry about him! It doesn't do any good, you know, husbands and wives worrying about each other."

"But you've got children."

"Children are a great worry," Mrs. Browning said confidentially. "Look at my big son over there. He's a worry to me. Yes, he is."

"Well, my dear lady, marry him off and get rid of him," Mr. Noyce said unctuously.

"Oh, you can talk! But I'd much better hold my tongue. I'm not used to this sort of company."

"Now, don't feel like that," Mr. Noyce said. "Look, I put you beside me because we don't often meet, and I wanted to get to know you."

"Well, I'm pleased, I'm sure."

When the mince-pies and the brandy-butter came in, and some bottles of champagne, Mrs. Ethelburger called out from the other end of the table, "Oh really! This is *too* much!"

Everyone laughed, except Mrs. Browning, who looked down at her plate and muttered, "Ill bred!" which Mr. Noyce heard.

"You're quite right," he said quietly, bending over her; "we all are. But you mustn't be such a snob, you know."

"Oh, you can laugh at me as much as you like, I'm not touchy. But I'm not such an old silly, either. Where I come from we knew how to deal with the likes of her! But I shouldn't have spoken."

"No, no; please do go on. This is very interesting."

"Fun's fun," Mrs. Browning said. "You're not getting any more out of me. See?"

"You're a very naughty old lady. Have some champagne?" Mr. Noyce said. But she put her hand over her glass.

Later on, towards the end of dinner, and after several glasses of champagne, Mrs. Noyce began to take an almost unmannerly interest in Mrs. Browning's son. Anything that her neighbour, Mrs. Ethelburger, said, she offered at once to her other neighbour, Mr. Browning. This caused some embarrassment, which she hadn't the wit to perceive. Finally the Rector engaged Mrs. Ethelburger in conversation, so Mrs. Noyce had Mr. Browning all to herself. She flirted with him, and he watched her drinking, uncomfortably, with a fixed smile on his face. There was no need for him to speak very much, she did all the talking. But he could not very well turn away. She switched the conversation suddenly to marriage.

"Now," he said, taking a mouthful of mince-pie and pausing to chew it, "now, I know what you're going to say! I ought to get married. That's what everybody says."

"Ah ha! But not me!" Mrs. Noyce said.

"Really?" Mr. Browning said. "Well, of course you are right. There's nobody left for me. All the beautiful women *are* married. That's what I always say."

"Yes, you are nice now (I really mustn't keep on saying 'nice,' must I. But I do think you are nice). But a man isn't at all nice after he's married. No. I tell you, what do you think of this? You needn't worry, my husband wouldn't care in the least. But just fancy calling me the Queen of the Wilis in the middle of the party. That's what he did. But I'm not, I'm not. I am poor Giselle."

"Oh, now, you mustn't feel like that," Mr. Browning said.

Very fortunately for him, Mrs. Darlington bent down and whispered something in her mistress's ear at that moment.

"Have you any idea what she's been talking about?" Mr. Browning said to Mr. Ethelburger, who had been silent for some time.

"Oh, these women—you know what they are," Mr. Ethelburger said.

Mr. Browning looked at him sharply, but he seemed bored rather than anything else.

"Well, the ladies are supposed to leave the gentlemen to it now, if you've all finished," Mrs. Noyce said, rising.

"Thank God," Mr. Browning said under his breath.

Mrs. Noyce and Mrs. Ethelburger found themselves alone in the drawing-room for a time while the others were upstairs.

"I've had far too much to drink," said Mrs. Noyce. "It's better here, though. I think Mr. Browning is charming, don't you?"

"Why ask me?" Mrs. Ethelburger said. "Personally I hate being kicked under the table. Did he try that on you too?"

Mrs. Noyce looked stunned.

"Sorry," Mrs. Ethelburger said. "I thought you were trying to be funny. Forget what I said. Yes, as men go, I suppose he is charming. But look here, for various reasons I don't want to be left alone with him. It's a long story—a family quarrel—that sort of thing. Rather difficult to explain. But be a dear, will you, and help me keep away from him. He's got a fearfully one-track mind, but that would be quite fun for you if you really do think he's charming."

"But, my dear, what an extraordinary thing! Who ever would think he's like that!" Mrs. Noyce said, opening her eyes very wide.

"I thought everyone knew that. Better not tell your husband, then," Mrs. Ethelburger said casually. "What a terrible bore men are, aren't they? And yet it's so dull without them, don't you agree? Pity we don't know each other rather more, otherwise I could ask you about your husband. You know, he's an interesting man, your husband, very interesting."

"Tell me just one thing," said Mrs. Noyce. "Is Mr. Browning at all, in the least, fond of you? Or has he ever been?"

"Is that going to worry you, or did you just ask because you thought I was being impertinent about your husband? I was, I know. But you gave me such a funny look, standing there before dinner, so sad, so terribly sad it seemed to me. And I've been wondering about you."

"About my husband."

"Oh no. I only meant how you feel about him. Some women love talking about their husbands, you know. And it does them good."

"Do you talk about your husband?"

"No. He wouldn't like it."

"Well, nor would mine."

"That's exactly what I wanted to know! You do mind that he minds. So really, you're all right, then." Mrs. Noyce lit a cigarette. "If you really want to know, I'm miserable," she said; "but there's nothing one can do about it."

"Well, for heaven's sake, don't imagine your happiness depends on men," Mrs. Ethelburger said. "If one happens to be the sort of woman men like, there's no need to get excited. And if not, it's too bad. That's all there is to it."

Mrs. Spark and Mrs. Browning came in then. "Ah! That's better!" Mrs. Spark said, warming her back at the fire. "These low-cut dresses are so chilly, aren't they? Tell me, how's your painting? I can't think how you manage with a big house like this to look after as well. Don't you find housekeeping a bit of a trial, Mrs. Browning?"

"I've done it all my life. And when you've always done it, well, it's just natural," Mrs. Browning said. "So true," said Mrs. Spark. "You look rather tired, Mrs. Ethelburger. It's that large family of yours, I dare say. But this is time off for you, isn't it? So you don't want to be reminded about that. And, my dear Mrs. Noyce, what an absolutely wonderful dinner you gave us!"

"You have my husband to thank for that. It was he who arranged it," Mrs. Noyce said.

"Really? I'm sure my husband couldn't even arrange our breakfast!"

"But breakfast is ever so much more difficult, isn't it really, when you come to think of it?" Mrs. Ethelburger said. "I mean, day after day, porridge without lumps and that sort of thing. And the milk boils over. But, of course, a man gives orders, he doesn't do the thing."

"Oh well, my dear, a man has his role, hasn't he? Just as we have ours."

"Of course. Yes. But quite apart from all that, I think they might help with the other necessary things."

"I'm not sure that I see what you mean."

"Well, you know, bees?"

"Bees?"

"Yes. Well, after the marriage flight the drone—"

But the men interrupted her, and she never explained. Mrs. Spark went over to Mrs. Browning and shook her head. "That sort of thing doesn't amuse me at all. Does it you?" she said.

"It beats me what a man—" Mrs. Browning began, but she shut her mouth on it.

"Oh, as for that. . . . It was the children I was wondering about really," said Mrs. Spark.

Mr. Browning went straight up to Mrs. Ethelburger. She looked as though she might get up, so he said, "Stay there. Listen, if you move, I shall follow you about. You've got to talk to me."

"What on earth about?" she said.

"Barbara, you know," he said.

"But isn't that all over?"

"That's not what I understood from your letter."

"Well, I've changed my mind. Things have changed."

"And you'll change it again."

"No."

"Yes!"

Mrs. Noyce, Mrs. Browning and Mr. Ethelburger all suddenly arrived on the scene at once. Everybody wanted to talk to Mr. Browning and Mrs. Ethelburger, it seemed. But what made it a little embarrassing was that when it came to the point, nobody said anything much. Mr. Noyce went over to see what was happening.

"Well, dear, I hope you haven't been drinking too much," Mrs. Spark said, left with her husband at the fireside.

"And what have you women been talking about?" he said.

"To tell you the truth, they were such a dull lot that I had to do all the talking!" Mrs. Spark said. "Whatever would Emm have to say if I told her that?"

"Well, now you really have something to say when you write," he said.

Meanwhile, Mr. Noyce had somehow or other managed to get everyone else out of the way, and, pouring a little rum in her coffee, spoke to Mrs. Ethelburger in his most soothing tone of voice. "You are a difficult person, aren't you?" he said. "Up one minute and down the next. Now what's upset you? You do look very upset."

As for Mr. Browning, he frowned at Mrs. Noyce, not listening to a word she said. Which was rude, because she was asking whether he would care to come with the others and see her painting. This had been Mr. Noyce's idea, she was only obeying instructions.

"I think I'll stay here and come up a bit later," Mrs. Ethelburger said, when the question was put to her. In the end she had her way. But, of course, Mr. Browning escaped from the rest after a decent interval. And now he faced her.

"I'm not going to beat about the bush," he said. "I think you are intolerable. The worst possible type of woman. Cunning and unfaithful. A bitch."

"Yes, well?" Mrs. Ethelburger said.

"That's all. And I hope you're as lonely as hell."

"Sorry about that letter," Mrs. Ethelburger said. "Oh, that's not going to catch me!"

"That's all right, then. I think someone is coming, so you'd better go now."

"The sooner the better."

"Lawrence!" Mrs. Browning called. "Lawrence—where are you? Come and help me down these stairs!"

It wasn't very warm in the studio. Mrs. Spark hunched her shoulders and peered at the pictures, waiting for Mr. Noyce to stop talking. She wanted her wrap, but didn't like to interrupt to ask for it, and as her husband seemed to be the only one listening to what Mr. Noyce said, it was only polite for her to remain silent. Mr. Noyce was talking about Art. First he discussed it in general terms, and then, when his wife and Mr. Ethelburger drifted into a corner and he only had Mr. Spark left (Mrs. Spark had never really counted because she went up to the paintings one by one, examining them all by herself, not waiting to be told what sort of thing to expect), he had become more personal, and spoke about style and the individual approach.

"Now you see here what Eileen is doing," he was saying, pointing out a landscape, "and, by the way, she has a wonderful palette—here she experiments with tone. Green is a pitfall, the most difficult colour of all for an artist. Well, here you see" (he covered up one half of the painting) "we have *this* sort of effect—cold, unsympathetic by itself. And her problem here has been to relate the green trees and grass and so on with the red farm wagons without violence." He took his hand away and stepped back beside Mr. Spark to examine the painting in less detail. "Yes," he said, "yes, I think it's come off, I think she's got it."

Mrs. Noyce smoked a cigarette, looking rather glum until Mr. Ethelburger said, "Fancy you doing this sort of thing! You're such a feminine sort of person."

Then she visibly brightened. "Nice to hear you talk like that," she said.

"What makes a person take up art, I wonder?" Mr. Ethelburger said.

"Oh, being wrong about everything else; being out of step. I don't know."

"A great thing to have a real interest. I often wish Barbara would take something up."

"She's got her children," Mrs. Noyce said. "She doesn't know how lucky she is. I'd love to have a real home like yours, and a family."

But Mr. Ethelburger didn't seem to be interested about this.

"Does anyone else in your family paint?" he asked. "I suppose there is an artistic tradition in your family. I know it made it much easier for me, my father being a farmer."

"Oh no, it wasn't that. I'm just a rebel," Mrs. Noyce said.

"A rebel? And what do you rebel against?"

"Society. Traditions and the family. Everything."

Mr. Ethelburger laughed. "It's always the same!" he said. "Why is it you women always want to have your cake and eat it? And you get away with it. Only, of course, you're angry about not having a family as well as everything else. No, honestly, Mrs. Noyce, you must admit you've made a pretty good thing out of rebellion, haven't you? But don't let it become a habit, or it might turn into one of those life-long grouses that women more than men do seem to get."

"I wish you'd call me Eileen," Mrs. Noyce said.

"She's rather too interested in technique, if you ask me," Mr. Noyce was saying, "and, of course, there is fashion in art. But if an artist paints fashionably for the sake of sales, he's damned. This lighting upsets the tone values, of course—still, it gives you an idea. Daylight lighting, you know, I had it put in myself."

"So very clever of you," Mrs. Spark said, going over to Mrs. Noyce in the corner. "I'm sure I'd never be able to do it in a thousand years. Tell me, which is the way to the bedroom, my dear, where we left our coats? When you're old like me, you begin to feel the cold."

"Yes, we are cut off here, I realise that," Mr. Noyce said to Mr. Spark. "Perhaps she ought to be more with her own sort. But, then, she's not a Bohemian character. And artists are queer, you know. More often than not they sit about and talk, and don't do any work when they get together. Still, there is that point. She could always go up to London, though, and see the exhibitions and keep in touch. I'm afraid we have rather lost touch with our friends. But where on earth are you all off to?"

Mrs. Noyce and Mrs. Spark and Mr. Ethelburger paused at the door.

"We're going down to get warm," Mrs. Noyce said.

"But, my dear, have they seen the pictures? You can't expect people to take it all in in a minute. You must let them *look*."

"It's all my fault," Mrs. Spark said.

"No, come on," said Mrs. Noyce. "We've all had quite enough. Come on, Harry, don't be a bore." She guided the other two out.

"Well!" Mr. Noyce said.

"Ha ha," said the Rector. "Don't you be bullied, my dear chap, she only meant it for a joke. Besides, Clare isn't really very artistic. Not keenly so, if you know what I mean. And I dare say Mr. Ethelburger has plenty of other things to worry about."

"A very beautiful woman, that wife of his," Mr. Noyce said. "Cigarette? Or what about another cigar?"

"No, thanks," Mr. Spark said. "You know, I think your wife is uncommonly gifted."

"Yes. But sometimes I wonder . . . Women don't seem to have the guts. I suppose we all want what we haven't got. And yet, you know, funnily enough, just to-day it came to me how fortunate I was—how right it was for me to be here. I felt that I belonged. Surely, after all these years you feel that too."

"When one's old—" the Rector began.

"No-no-no-no. Not that way," Mr. Noyce said. "It's deep down inside. 'Man shall not live by bread alone,' as you might say. Perhaps it's only imagination, but I suddenly felt how satisfactory it was to have roots, to be entwined in a place, to be nourished. And I have travelled a lot in my day. Of course, it's difficult for Eileen to understand it. But then a woman ought to be able to take over her husband's place and make it her own. Or do women ever belong?"

"Sharing an interest—really that's what matters, isn't it?" the Rector said. "And you two certainly do that."

Mr. Noyce looked surprised.

"Painting," the Rector said.

"Oh, she won't share *that*. Good heavens, no. She *does*n't. I'm just one of those extraordinary creatures who are interested in art—which couldn't be more different, I assure you. There's nothing like the contempt of an artist for ordinary mortals. And should you attempt to criticise— God help you. But, you see, I just don't take any notice.

And the only reason we haven't parted company (oh, I'm not giving away secrets, don't look so worried) is because I have got a sincere admiration for people who create."

"And of course you write, don't you?"

"I always hoped my *nom de plume* would shelter me."

"But now why? They are lovely imaginative stories. I gave them to my nieces last year for Christmas, and am told they were much appreciated."

"I dare say, I dare say. But, please, if you don't mind, keep quiet about my being the author."

"Oh, I say—why?"

"Because, damn it—well, if a man bothers to use a *nom de plume*, he means it, doesn't he?"

After this there was a long silence, and then Mr. Noyce said, "Well, let's go and see what they're all up to. I suppose we ought to organise a game of bridge or something." He looked at his watch.

Downstairs Mr. Browning was doing conjuring tricks, while Mrs. Spark applauded and Mrs. Noyce watched. His mother kept on looking round from her place at the table beside him to try and see if the Ethelburgers were interested. They sat a little apart, near the fire. "I don't care, it was damn rude of you," Mr. Ethelburger was saying very quietly to Mrs. Ethelburger.

"But why should I trudge up all those stairs just to look at some paintings?" she said.

"Because you're a guest here."

"Only because you said it would be good for me."

"Really! Must we go all over that again?"

"No. Not if you shut up about being polite."

"Well, I do think it was shockingly rude."

"All right then, I'll go now."

"Barbara—stop making an exhibition of yourself!"

But it was too late, she had already got up.

She went over to the table and whispered in Mrs. Noyce's ear. "Just off to have a look at the pictures, my dear. Don't bother now, but John's in a bad mood and wants cheering up. Shan't be long."

Mr. Browning made a bad mess of the knotted handkerchief.

"There now!" Mrs. Spark said. "We've caught him out!"

"It's ever so long since he's done it. He doesn't get enough practice, you see," Mrs. Browning said. "Besides, it's no good if you're interrupted."

"Sorry! Sorry!" Mrs. Ethelburger called out, moving off.

Mrs. Browning breathed in a waft of Chanel Numero Cinque and said no more.

Mr. Noyce and the Rector were half-way down the stairs when they met Mrs. Ethelburger round the bend coming up. "Just going to have a look at the paintings," she explained, when they courteously made way for her.

"Oh, I see," Mr. Noyce said. "Come along then, I'll take you up."

"Well, I think I'll go along down, if you don't mind," the Rector said.

Mr. Noyce turned the daylight lighting on. "There!" he said.

"How ghastly," said Mrs. Ethelburger. "Better than those things in the streets, though. They make you look bright yellow."

"Not interested in painting, are you?" Mr. Noyce said.

"Not when they're all made sickly by a blue light."

"Yes, it's true. I told them that."

"Let me off and I'll come and see them in the day."

"Good idea." Mr. Noyce turned the light off. "Well," he said. "What shall we do now? What are they doing with themselves downstairs?"

"Mr. Browning is being frightfully clever with conjuring tricks."

"Oh, God!"

"I know. But he has to be like that."

They began walking downstairs again.

"The trouble is," Mr. Noyce said, "Eileen's such a damn rotten hostess. Any normal person would have seen what was coming and fairly stamped on those conjuring tricks. But she's hopeless."

"I think she's awfully nice," Mrs. Ethelburger said. "But probably she's nice because you're beastly to her, if you see what I mean. Not awfully good for you, though."

"Wait a minute. Let's walk down slowly," Mr. Noyce said. "It's fun talking to you. And as I keep on saying this evening, you are so beautiful."

"That's because you've been drinking," Mrs. Ethelburger said. "*Must* we go back and be bored by those people?"

Mr. Noyce looked at his watch again. "Ten o'clock," he said. "Well, we'll have a quarter of an hour off, shall we? It isn't quite time for anyone to say they want to go yet. And, after all, to each is given what defeat he will. It's not my fault if people put up with conjuring tricks."

They went into the study, where it was still warm although the fire had gone out.

"This is where I work," Mr. Noyce said.

"Oh yes. You write children's books," Mrs. Ethelburger said.

"So you know, too!"

"Yes. I bought them for my kids when Mrs. Spark told me. But they're much more for grown-ups really, aren't they? I read them sometimes by myself. They comfort me. But of course the modern child—well, that's another thing."

"Really," Mr. Noyce said. "Really. How interesting. Come and sit down."

"Yes, I'd love to," said Mrs. Ethelburger. "I'm just starting another one, I think, and all this standing about is rather a trial."

"Another one? Oh dear. . . ."

"It's quite all right, it was meant. Or don't you approve of women having babies?"

"Oh no, not at all. I mean, you are perfectly right," Mr. Noyce said. "It's because I am old-fashioned, I suppose, but I'm not used to people being so frank."

"Well, another time when a woman says no to your sherry, don't keep on. You see, pregnant women are sometimes sick. You do live with your head in the clouds here, don't you?" said Mrs. Ethelburger, gazing round at all the books.

"I suppose in a way I do," Mr. Noyce said; "and that's why a person like you is a breath of fresh air to me. You interest me terribly. How is it a beautiful woman like you can bury herself in the country when she might, with confidence, live anywhere else in any sort of society? Don't tell me it's love."

"Well, there is that," Mrs. Ethelburger said, "and don't forget mother. You see, I was one of the girls once. Not too particular so long as I had a good time. But what a bore it was! Golly, those men. My father always went bankrupt, you know; so there was never enough money for me to be properly brought up. So I never learned much. All that putting the world in order, mastering the havoc, history and so on. No, I never had that. And perhaps not being educated properly does make one notice things. How everyone exploits everyone else, for instance. And I was at the wrong end—pretty, young and careless, with no great big father asking 'What are your intentions, young man?' And absolutely no money. My dear old grandfather, a landed gent, you know, who often looked after me while mother ran about trying to retrieve father, didn't believe in careers for girls, and I never have liked work, much— who does? But grandad never made a will; so when he died the whole thing went to father, who immediately sold it up. You do see, don't you, what a problem it was? For the others, too, as well as me, I suppose. And it soon dawned on me that I should have to look after mother. Well, and then there was love. I still can't believe why anyone should love me. A queer thing, love. Nothing to do with being beautiful—many men have called me that. And I certainly don't try to please or put myself out. But sometimes I'm awfully happy. I think perhaps it must be that. After all, physical passion wouldn't have lasted, would it? And very soon, after all these ghastly babies, I shall really be respectable and look ugly."

"Look here," Mr. Noyce said. "I think you're so wonderful that I feel I simply must give you something—a sort of offering to one human being from another. Or a libation to some goddess. Isn't there some extraordinary, rare drink that pregnant women crave? Because I have a wonderful cellar."

"Well, I can always drink brandy," Mrs. Ethelburger said.

"Oh, you make me so happy," Mr. Noyce said. "You couldn't have chosen better. Look!"

He went over to a small cupboard, opened it, and took out a glass and an aged-looking bottle of brandy. "Not that I'm a secret drinker, you know," he said, offering the glass to Mrs. Ethelburger.

"Nor am I," she said. "But it's lovely, isn't it? Brandy, I mean."

"I tell you what," Mr. Noyce said, actually flushed with generosity, "I'll send you up a bottle of this, I've got two more. Just to tide you over, as it were. After all, it's going to be a difficult time, isn't it, till the baby is born?"

"Well, I shouldn't do that really," she said.

"Of course, of course—your husband—"

"No, it's mother. You see father drank and still does, and she's always afraid I might take after him."

"I could always put a cider label on the bottle."

"Not possible really, is it? You know, you do live in a dream."

Meanwhile the sort of conversation which precedes departure had begun in the drawing-room.

"I do think it's been a splendid party," Mrs. Spark said. "Now, you will let us have some of those wonderful chrysanthemums of yours for the Harvest Festival, won't you, Mr. Browning?"

"Wonderful weather, you know, we've had this year,'" Mr. Spark said to Mr. Ethelburger. "Of course it's even more important to you than to me. I wish you'd come down one day and give me some tips about my garden. I'd like to have a few words with you one day. But one can't really talk at these parties. How's time getting on, by the way?"

"What about another drink—something to keep you warm?" Mrs. Noyce said.

"Oh, it's not cold. I can give anyone a lift who wants one," Mr. Browning said.

"Yes, I really think we must go now," said Mrs. Spark. "Arthur?"

"Yes. Well, Mrs. Noyce, thank you ever so much for that wonderful dinner you gave us. Where's that husband of yours? We mustn't forget to congratulate him on his cellar."

"I'll just go and find him," Mrs. Noyce said.

She went out into the hall and called, "Harry! Harry!"

Nurse came out of her room. "I think he's gone in the study with one of the guests, Miss Eileen."

"Well, then, fetch him. And tell him he's keeping all his other guests waiting," Mrs. Noyce said.

Everything was tidied up in the kitchen. Mrs. Walmby drank a glass of stout with Mrs. Darlington, who was dressed to go, and the two girls, Linda and Irene, were putting their scarves on in the passage between the kitchen and the front hall. They could see through the baize door as they leant against the wall without being seen themselves if they hid behind the old mackintoshes and coats which always hung in the passage there; the spring on the hinge of the baize door had never been properly adjusted, and the door never quite shut. They watched the guests depart.

"Funny, aren't they, the way they hang about," Linda said.

"Look, doesn't he look smart. I've never seen him like that," said Irene.

"All smiles," said Linda. "You don't often see them like that."

"It's a bit like the pictures. But not so smart. And they take such a time. Ooh, look at that! He's kissing my Missus's hand!"

"Didn't know they did that, did you?" said Linda.

"Of course they do, silly. That's what they do on the pictures."

"But why, Rene? He's not doing it to the others."

"It's because she's a lady, that's why," Irene said.

Mrs. Noyce shut the front door.

"Well, that's that. Thank God!" she said.

"Oh, come now, Eileen, you can't say you didn't enjoy it," Mr. Noyce said.

Mrs. Noyce looked very angry indeed.

"Don't say it!" Mr. Noyce said. "My mistake. Let's go to bed."

"Harry," Mrs. Noyce said, "I'm going to leave you. Do you hear? I've had enough. I've made up my mind, I—"

"Not just now, Eileen. It's so late. And it's so draughty here. Let's leave all this till the morning, would you mind awfully?" Mr. Noyce said.

"I don't care how late it is, or anything else. I'm going. You understand?"

"Well, no. Unless you're going to walk. There aren't any trains till to-morrow, you know."

"Trains!" Mrs. Noyce said.

"Yes. I'll get the time-table if you like. I'm pretty sure there's nothing to-night."

"Ooh!" Irene said behind the baize door. She slipped away. But Linda stayed.

Mrs. Noyce turned her back on her husband and went upstairs. He stood looking at the floor for a moment, and then suddenly strode across the hall and flung open the baize door. He reached for his old coat, took it down. And then saw Linda.

"Hullo," he said. "What are you doing here? Don't goggle at me like that, you silly little girl."

"Oh," Linda said.

Mr. Noyce put his coat back on the peg. "Come along," he said. "I'm going to talk to you. We'll go to the drawing-room, it's warm in there. You know the way."

He made her sit down by the fire. The room still smelt of scent and drink and tobacco smoke. Chairs stood pushed back from the table, or in couples where people had finished talking and got up and suddenly left or wandered away. There were glasses and coffee-cups all over the place, and someone had dropped a handkerchief.

All the lights were on and the fire burned steadily. Linda kept on looking round.

"It's all right," Mr. Noyce said. "They won't come back. Funny how people alter a room, isn't it? It's not the same after they've gone. But this room is used to parties. In fact, cleaned up and put straight it hasn't any character at all. Would you like to have a drink?"

"No, thank you."

"Well, now, perhaps you'll tell me what this is all about. This spying and making up stories. You'll come to a bad end, you know, if you go on like that. Don't you know that it's queer to behave like that? Why do you do it?"

"I don't know," Linda said.

"You want to be important or something. Is that it?"

"I don't know."

"You would like to be someone, like my wife, would you?"

"Oh, I don't know."

"Try not to keep on saying that. Well, you heard what she said just now, didn't you?"

"Oh, no."

"It's hopeless. Poor little thing," Mr. Noyce said. He lit a cigarette.

"Look," he said, "try to imagine what it's like to be old like me. Look at my white hairs. I ought to be wise, oughtn't I? Well, then, listen to me. I've known plenty of silly little girls just like you, only they were brought up differently, so they didn't behave in quite such a dotty way. But they made a nuisance of themselves, just like you, chasing after some wretched man and making his life a misery, until something really horrid happened to them. And that stopped them being so silly. If it wasn't too late, they settled down and married and had lots of children. But quite a lot of them came to a bad end. You see?"

"What happened?"

"Nothing at all nice. It really isn't for me to tell you the facts of life. Do you read books? Novels and things?"

"Oh no. Mum wouldn't let me."

"Lying again. Well, look here. This is the last time you ever come to this house. Understand? It's not punishment for anything you've done, and I shan't tell your mother about how I caught you just now. So all you've got to do is keep your mouth shut, and you won't get a beating from your father. As I am never going to see you again, I hope, I would like to know if there's anything, just one thing I could do to help. Because I am sorry for you, and if I could, I would like to help. Now what is it you want to be or want to do? How do you honestly really think of yourself as you want yourself to be? Try to tell me, and don't say, 'I don't know'."

"Oh, I don't know. I'm sure I don't," Linda said. "But I don't want to be with Dad and Mum. And I don't want to be like the other girls. They're silly, if you like. I want to be different, see?"

"But, my dear child, everybody is like that—everybody thinks they want to be different from everyone else! You are just an ordinary rather stupid little girl. Run along now. Your mother will be wondering what's happened to you. And I'm sorry I can't help. I am, really."

"Nobody asked you to, I'm sure," Linda said.

After Linda had gone, Mr. Noyce stayed by the fire, smoking and thinking. Nurse found him like this when she came in to put the lights out.

"Come along, Master Harry," she said; "it's getting ever so late."

"That child Linda," he said; "she's an unfortunate, isn't she?"

"She's a little baggage," nurse said. "Whatever makes you think of her?"

"Well, one can't help wondering when one comes across people like that. It's so unfair. I mean, she can't possibly get away with it in her walk of life. She has what one calls the romantic temperament."

"I wouldn't call it that. I'd call it something else," nurse said.

"Naturally you would. Well, it can't be helped. You know, I've enjoyed myself this evening, thoroughly enjoyed myself," Mr. Noyce said. "It was a good party. Which reminds me, you haven't seen my wife about the place, have you?"

"No, Master Harry."

"Oh, good, then," said Mr. Noyce. "I expect, after all, she's just gone to bed."

Chapter Eleven

"The trivial round, the common task, will furnish all we need to ask," Mrs. Ethelburger was fond of saying while she stirred the porridge, made the toast and so on. Said like that, it sounded doubtful, but for the majority who sing it in church with a cheerful voice, it does hold true. Which is a good thing, because ordinary life is uneventful and consists of doing the necessary things over and over again and feeling pleased about it. Especially in winter life is apt to slow down to the trivial round level (I am not talking about life in towns where it is possible and even advisable not to take any notice of the weather, and where seasonal changes are noticed, chiefly, indoors where the central-heating is either turned on or not yet turned on). One appreciates the good sense of animals that go in for hibernation at this time. And how pleasant to pile up on top of a stove, for instance, which Russian peasants used to do (so one read), though it is doubtful whether they still do it now. But numbed with cold in horrible, draughty houses, with the plumbing all outside, the country dweller carries on. Starting with a cold in the head which removes the sense of taste and smell and makes one deaf and generally stupid, the advance of winter is heralded as well by gloomy fogs which hang about day after day, keeping the children indoors and rendering the roads impossible for traffic. Sensible people, recognising the state of affairs, keep the fires burning and read novels in their spare time, or sew and knit. The men grumble a lot, and come in and out with dirty boots and dogs (which smell like burning blankets when they try to get dry, bellies up, by the fire), and the children play with and break whatever toys are still with them from the Christmas before. Little things, such as the Siamese cat having Siamese kittens for once, or on the dark side, the house cow going suddenly dry, make all the difference one way or the other. But just as one can't work up any vivid enthusiasms, so one doesn't absolutely lose one's temper. Nothing starry eyed, no going off the deep end; life is at a low ebb.

Mrs. Ethelburger passed the time away with her feet up by the fire, making party dresses for the children. She had to do this because the everyday clothes the children wore were unsuitable for parties, and they had absolutely grown out of all the things she made last year. Mr. Ethelburger insisted that his children should go to parties, and even compelled his wife to organise a children's party of her own once a year. He of course dressed up as Father Christmas on these occasions, and it was after this that the Siamese generally had kittens on the remains of his cotton-wool beard. Christmas and the parties were not yet, however. These were the dull days before invitations were received and sent out, before even the Christmas pudding was made or Christmas presents seriously thought about. While Mrs. Ethelburger made the party clothes, her mother knitted. After the children had gone to bed, you would find them like that; Mrs. Ethelburger with her feet up on the sofa, Mrs. Flint in an armchair very near to the fire. Later, when Mr. Ethelburger came in, the sofa and the armchair were moved back and the cats moved off (to get up on things), while the dogs took the places where they had been until someone noticed the smell and drove them away from the fire. Mr. Ethelburger liked to read the papers then. First the *Daily Mirror*, then the *News Chronicle*, and lastly *The Times*. Or on Sunday, the *Sunday Times*. If the women had read the papers they were, of course, inside out and back to front (sometimes the middle page of *The Times* was actually *upside down*). This always upset Mr. Ethelburger. But most often no one but he ever read the papers. After reading the papers, he turned the wireless on for the news. And while the news was on Mr. Ethelburger read *The Farmers' Livestock* or *I Bought a Mountain*—a book he was particularly fond of and read over and over again, so the women chatted in low voices if the news was dull, till the next item on the programme, when the wireless was turned off. Then, either they went on chatting in louder voices and Mr. Ethelburger read on, or else Mrs. Ethelburger said something beginning with "Look, John," and for a short time he would enter into the conversation. One could see that later on in life he was the sort of person who would fall asleep after dinner in his chair. But that, too, is not yet.

Mr. Noyce's party, coming as it did on the threshold of winter, was a godsend in the homes of the invited, both before and after it was held. In fact, it was something fresh to talk about for at least three months, if you count the time before as well as after. It is lowering and bad for the nerves when women have nothing to talk about except the weather in the evenings. Silence in women is not golden, but lead which plumbs the depths. Imagine, then, the stories about what Mrs. Spark wore, the spray which Mr. Browning gave her, getting wilder and wilder, and the dinner, surprising in any case, passing over into the realm of legend. And Mrs. Browning's necklace, and Mrs. Noyce's jewellery—each home had something to enlarge upon. But no one else had an audience like Mrs. Flint. Over and over again Mrs. Ethelburger told her the story of the party until in the end, even Mr. Ethelburger became interested.

"What on earth are you talking about, Barbara?" he said one evening. And was amazed when told they were speaking about the party.

"But it's just not true," he said.

"Oh yes," Mrs. Flint said. "I know exactly what Barbara means. Backless, with a taffeta slip under black lace—just like the dresses they used to wear."

"But, damn it all, I was there," Mr. Ethelburger said. Which made no difference, because as soon as he started to read the women were back at it again.

Emm got any number of letters. She answered these in a firm hand, dealing with the shortcomings of the Middle Classes in a way that did much to console her sister, who would remark, "Of course, it is so different seeing things from on top. I mean, we as a family have always had a sense of proportion, we never had to bother about Class."

"Well, well," said the Rector, "I'm glad, though, you keep in touch with Emm. Writing letters is an art, and it does seem to make you happy."

Mrs. White, who would gladly have been an audience for Mrs. Spark, was told the proper things for her to know, and found out little more because she was unable to work and listen at the same time, and Mrs. Spark always kept the conversation short. Mr. Browning and the Rector talked endlessly about gardening when they met, so the subject of the party was kept fresh between Mrs. Browning and her son. She was getting very old. To her it seemed that winter was an endless time. Her bones ached and she moved about slower and slower, grumbling to herself, but always keeping the house extremely clean, and worrying about dust behind cupboards which the brush couldn't reach. To her son she said shocking things like, "*I'll* never see another summer. May as well make up your mind to it." But in her heart she never gave in. And when an old man of eighty who lived in one of the Almshouses died, she went to his funeral and said afterwards quite cheerfully, "Well, *he* won't have to bother about any more green Christmases." She often went to the graveyard. One day she met Mr. Noyce there. He was standing with his arms akimbo, looking at his parents' grave. It was one of the fenced-in sort, but the weeds had grown so rank behind the iron rails that the tombstone with its trumpeting angel on top could hardly be seen at all.

"Hullo, you naughty old lady, how are you getting on?" Mr. Noyce said. Mrs. Browning came up beside him then.

"Fancy you remembering," she said. "It seems ever such a time ago, that party. What's written on there?"

"Oh, Peace, Perfect Peace, or something. To tell you the truth, I forget."

"No, his age. It is your father's, isn't it?"

"Yes. He was eighty-four. And mother was eighty."

"Oh, I shall never be that! They've beaten me, then," Mrs. Browning said. She looked rather sad.

"Cheer up," Mr. Noyce said. "Anyway, what are you doing here? Choosing a plot?"

Mrs. Browning cackled and made a pass at him with her stick. "I'm not thinking of lying down beside them with me toes up yet," she said. "Though it is hard, with the rheumatism and the cold that makes your bones ache. Still, they can't feel anything at all down there. So I'm one better than them, anyway."

"Yes, I suppose it comes to that," Mr. Noyce said. And he, too, looked sad.

Ever since the party Mr. Noyce had been feeling sad. On and off he had even thought of taking to his bed. But the thought of a doctor and possibly a nurse which this course of inaction conjured up was such a worry that instead he played chess with himself and tried to make up crossword puzzles. Otherwise he worked at his children's stories and kept his diary, and walked about on his estate in the fog. On one of these occasions (just after the fog had cleared a bit), he had caught Mr. Broom with a pheasant under his arm and a gun. It was a Sunday and he hadn't ordered any game. There was no excuse. He hadn't given Broom notice, he was feeling far too sad to do that, but naturally a coldness had sprung up between them, and one more ideal was shattered. One by one his wife had shattered the others. Strange how a proud man like Mr. Noyce depended so much on ideals, which in others he most likely would only have found amusing.

"The master's beginning to be old," Mrs. Walmby said to nurse one morning over their cup of tea. "Yesterday he never touched his apple-tart and didn't even notice when the fire was out."

"It's sorrow, not old age," nurse said, "and we all know who's to blame for that." Mrs. Noyce she meant, of course.

Mrs. Noyce was having the time of her life. Far from living the dull, quiet, country existence I have taken so much trouble to describe, she spent most of her time in London, paying a round of visits to her old friends and being a great success. She was having a splendid time. It had happened like this. About a week after the party (she had not left her husband that night or the next morning—he had never believed that she would) Mrs. Noyce had a letter from someone who had once bought a picture of hers.

In the normal course of events she would have shown this letter to her husband because it came from a person on the business side of the art world, and had to do with the sort of arrangements that Mr. Noyce, not she, was supposed to understand. But because it came at the tail end of a quarrel, at a very low moment when there seemed nothing else to do but start patching things up, Mrs. Noyce, filled with a sense of the injustice of all that she had been made to suffer, sat down in her studio and answered the letter herself. And then, feeling that true independence needed more obvious action, she had followed up the letter with a visit to London in person.

"Another time do let us know when you're coming back," Mr. Noyce said at dinner, just after her return. He sighed and cut the partridge in half.

"No, no, I'm not a bit hungry. I'll just have some cheese," Mrs. Noyce said.

Mr. Noyce put the half back on his plate. "Just as you like," he said.

She had meant to keep her adventures a surprise, letting out casually over coffee after dinner that someone—quite an intelligent man who, incidentally, had once bought a picture of hers; he was a collector of contemporary work—had written to ask whether she had done any more painting lately, and if so, was she showing in

London at all? He knew some people who were. It was a pity to hide one's light under a bushel. He had a friend, an art critic, who thought a lot of her work, had enjoyed her earlier exhibition. (True enough, Mrs. Noyce had once held an exhibition of her pictures; it had not been a financial success. Mr. Noyce, who had arranged it all, had been quite prepared to stand the loss.) But eating bread and cheese in silence while he ate the partridge was more than Mrs. Noyce could stand. All of a sudden she said:

"Harry, I'm going to have a show in London. With some others. It's just been settled. We've got it all arranged. Mine are being hung—"

"Eileen," Mr. Noyce said, "you're being stupid. You know how stupid it is to do things like this. Now just tell me quite quietly, if you can, what exactly you have done."

Then she had told him how the pictures she had taken with her had been praised, not only by her patron but by her patron's friend, the critic who wrote about art for the evening papers. How there was a feeling in the air for a new movement—a fresh feeling for the understanding of the arts—she had felt it herself, and so had all the other painters. And lastly she told him about the art gallery which, although not in the most fashionable part of London, was sure to be crowded because the critic with his personal enthusiasm for the venture was bound to draw attention there.

"And who is this critic? Who are these other artists? And who the hell is going to *pay* for it all?" Mr. Noyce said.

In an exasperated, quiet voice Mrs. Noyce told him that all men ever thought about was money.

He had asked too many leading questions. He saw his mistake and tried to put things in a reasonable way. He told her what would happen, how she hadn't done enough work yet to hold another exhibition; how either success or failure was bound to upset her, and how a real artist, who was sheltered and fed must work and work and work. But in vain. So Mrs. Noyce had packed up the rest of her pictures and gone to London again.

As things turned out, the exhibition was quite a success. Mrs. Noyce had her own personal triumph, with good write-ups and her picture in an evening paper, wearing a rather nice hat. She even sold three of her paintings, though this did not pay for the trips to London. Now there was no need for Mr. Noyce to tell his wife to put on lots of jewellery and make up her face. Besides which, she spent an awful lot of money on clothes, and every time she came home, which was about once a week at first but got less (she wrote, though), she demanded more and more money. And if there was one thing Mr. Noyce really hated, it was quarrelling about money. So he gave her cheques, and then worried a few days, and then realised a bit more capital, and then thought about taking to his bed.

"You're jealous, that's what you are, you don't like me being a success," Mrs. Noyce said to him once. It sounds more unkind than it actually was. He had told her that she now looked like a second-rate actress past her prime, instead of "a practically unknown artist" as the papers said. But it's no use making excuses. And no use for him to say, "Not that sort of success. I saw in you a real artist;" no use all his warnings, all his protests. And no use being humble either; that was a mistake.

"No. You see, you didn't want me when I was here," Mrs. Noyce said. "So even if you did sell this place, we couldn't live together."

Another time he said, "But, Eileen, where are you going to paint in London?"

"Oh, to hell with that," she said.

At this, the final shattering of his ideals, he told her all the things men do tell women who have hurt their feelings—a terribly long description of suffering and privation, the punishment a man takes looking on while all this happens, the poor view the world takes of a certain kind of woman, and at last, the sting in the tail, "And when you find out how right I am, it will be too late. It won't be the slightest good your coming back to me then." So foolish, because all the talk of punishment and sorrow might have touched her heart, but she was bound to get tough after that. Still, only a foolish woman would have let such a scene happen without first having made her mind up.

Only the really hard-hearted are never foolish, I think, when it comes to affairs of the heart. Perhaps 'amour propre' is a more appropriate expression than 'love' to describe the emotions I am dealing with here. Is there such a thing as disinterested love? I would say, yes, there is.

Very few women leave their husbands without having another man within reach. Even then, old habits, old ways of thought are hard to break.

"Harry, we can't part like this," Mrs. Noyce said the next day. (She couldn't go the night before as, again, there were no trains.)

"We certainly can't go on as we are," Mr. Noyce said. "In any case, do let's have breakfast in peace. Coffee?"

"Yes, please. I feel I have behaved rather badly."

Her husband said nothing, so she went on, "I'll pay back that money."

"Oh?" Mr. Noyce said.

"Yes. And of course I shall go on painting. But there are other things which come first."

"Then you'll never be able to paint. And that is why there are no great artists among your sex."

"It's no good talking. You just don't understand," Mrs. Noyce said.

"Shall I order a taxi?" Mr. Noyce said after breakfast.

"Oh, Harry, don't you care if I go? I didn't mean it to be like this."

"Look here," Mr. Noyce said. "I've had enough. What do you think I've been doing for the last three weeks? Trying to kick you out? And now when you've made it perfectly clear that you *are* going, whatever I say, you still want me to make a fuss. Oh, do go away."

By the time the taxi arrived, Mr. Noyce had shut himself up in the study. But Mrs. Noyce felt she couldn't go off like that. She knocked at the door.

"Harry, I'm going," she said.

"Good-bye," said Mr. Noyce.

She went in.

"Oh, you have done such a lot for me, really you have. And I am grateful," she said. "Whatever happens, do believe that."

"Don't be sickening," Mr. Noyce said.

"But, Harry, I may not come back!"

"Good," Mr. Noyce said. "Well, I hope you have a lovely time. You'll miss that train, if you don't hurry up."

And so, in tears, Mrs. Noyce went away. The mascara got into her eyes, as it always does when you weep, but it was quite a long way to the station, which gave her time to get herself straight.

It is generally true that the one who is left suffers more than the one who goes away—at any rate, at first. But I am not yet quite up to date. Two days before Mr. Noyce met Mrs. Browning in the church-yard, Mrs. Noyce came down from London again. It was only to take her clothes and personal things away and to ask for a divorce. Perhaps because Mr. Noyce was really rather old-fashioned, he was shocked about this. Mrs. Noyce, whose thoughts by now were on other things, who, in every sense, moved in another world, was slightly irritated when he said, "But, Eileen, you understand what this means?" There's nothing like a woman started out on a new life for the brief matter-of-fact method which she uses to deal with the old. Perhaps it's to do with all that house-keeping business in the blood—turning out last year's rubbish or the nest-building instinct, a powerful forward-looking idea—I don't know. Anyway, Mrs. Noyce said, "Don't be such an owl. What else *could* all this mean? You'll get an hotel bill. And, Harry, do get on with it."

Unhappy he certainly was, but Mr. Noyce was not the kind to sit about waiting for hotel bills, and he decided that evening to do something at last about the state of his parents' grave. Of the happenings I have described, the village so far knew nothing beyond the fact that Mrs. Noyce was often away. But some time or other they would find out, and this would not be very pleasant for Mr. Noyce. Never for a moment, though, did he consider leaving. Indeed, looking after the grave was an outward and visible sign of the pledge he made to himself that he belonged here and would not go. Through the Rector he got Mr. White to help him remove some of the railings, and together they cleared the weeds.

"You want a nice bit of marble now. That's what you want," Mr. White said when the job was finished.

"No," Mr. Noyce said. "Flowers. And I'll have those railings taken away."

Mr. White was deaf, so he said nothing. But of course flowers were a bit of a problem in winter.

"You can't have flowers *now*," the Rector said when consulted. So in the end Mr. Noyce's gardener planted a lot of bulbs, and rabbits ate them. It doesn't sound much, but all this took Mr. Noyce's mind off his other worries.

"What an ignorant fellow he is!" the Rector said to his wife. "Good gracious, with that garden of his, one would have thought he could see that there are very few winter flowers."

"Typically bourgeois," Mrs. Spark said. "Exploiting the people. Never done a day's honest work himself. Living in the midst of plenty—"

"Clare, Clare, all those are platitudes. Besides," the Rector said, "whatever you may think of Mr. Noyce, he comes of a very old and respected family. If he belongs to the bourgeoisie, then so do you, my dear."

"I know what you are driving at, Arthur. But you see, unlike you, I wasn't brought up with all these class prejudices. My family were once rulers, but whatever purpose did these landed gentry serve? Greedy landlords, that's what they are!"

"My dear, as I've said before, I don't think you quite understand what you are talking about. If you really want to be a Communist, you should first of all read *Das Kapital*. It's somewhere about in the library."

Mrs. Spark drummed her fingers on the table, smiling a bit, but not looking at her husband.

"Arthur," she said, "to be a good Comrade doesn't mean that one has to be so awfully clever. You, for instance, are an intellectual. But the really important people, you know, are the Workers."

The Rector sighed.

Still, ever since Mrs. Spark had learnt to sing 'The Red Flag' she had been much happier. She caught the bus every Wednesday afternoon (early closing day in the town), and stayed on for the factory workers' meeting. She read Communist tracts, and had ordered the *Daily*

Worker. (But for some reason it had never come.) She carried on with her Women's Institute activities just as usual and arranged the flowers for Sunday services, and, in fact, carried on in every way just the same. Only every now and then there were these little outbursts. It made the Rector careful with what he said. But one cannot always think twice before one speaks, and so there were collisions. There are many surprising things about married life, but the apparent ease with which two people even in their old age can settle down to a new phase in their relationship is surely one of the most extraordinary. Before, it had always been the Rector who was right about everything; he held the magic keys. Now they were obsolete. Not that Mrs. Spark had stopped being a Christian—far from it—she often remarked how near she felt to those early Christians (about A.D. 1). It was in her attitude to the little vexations—politics, what sort of books to put down on the library list, what programmes to listen to on the wireless—the sort of things a puzzled wife refers to her husband with confidence in his superior powers, that Mrs. Spark had changed. He was quite calm about it all, and except for one thing (barring the arguments, of course, but they were only tiffs), never showed any strong feelings about the change. But instead of presenting her with a bunch of roses on her birthday as usual, he gave her a book on dialectical materialism. It proves, I think, that women are hard to please, because she was very hurt.

Mrs. Browning had spent a good deal of time trying to persuade her son not to have a party when he said he wanted to give one, but, used to him having his way in these matters, she was surprised as well as relieved when he suddenly gave in and said, "You are perfectly right, Mother. It would be a farce. I can't go one better than him. Besides, these days I haven't the energy."

"You know, you do look bad," his mother said. "I've been noticing it these last days."

"Oh, don't fuss," Mr. Browning said.

He asked the Rector down to drink a glass of sherry with him. They sat in the ingle-nook by the fire—it was too cold now on the verandah, and of course quite dark by six o'clock.

"Forgive me for being personal," the Rector said, "but honestly, you don't look well."

"I'm a sick man," Mr. Browning said.

"Well, then, what about a doctor?"

"I can't stick doctors. None of them has ever done me any good. I'm a sick man, I know that. But I'm not going to give in."

"This is sheer foolishness," the Rector said. "Look here—"

"Oh, I know all the arguments. But I'll take what's coming, thank you. Have another drink?"

Afterwards the Rector spoke to Mrs. Browning while her son was getting the car out. "You know, you simply must persuade him to see a doctor," he said. "It might very well be something serious. I don't want to alarm you, but it gave me a shock to see him like that."

"It's no good you telling me to persuade him. It's his head. He never sees a doctor till he's laid flat. He's always been like that," Mrs. Browning said.

Although the Rector lived quite near, Mr. Browning had insisted on driving him home in his car.

"I would like to have thrown a party, you know," he said, as they went up the hill. "But honestly, what is the good of all this showing off and going one better? For that's what it amounts to. Look here, I know I could succeed in throwing the hell of a party if I tried. It's pointless, though. Sometimes I feel I've tried everything and nothing's any good. One shouldn't feel like that. Bad, isn't it?"

"It's the time of year," the Rector said. "Very depressing weather."

"But the time of year and the weather is life. No good making a fuss about winter when it comes." They drove between the chestnut trees, and the Rectory came in sight. "I say, do come in," the Rector said. "Come and have a chat with my wife. She's full of new ideas—it might cheer you up!" But Mr. Browning refused the invitation, and drove quickly back home to get on with his work. "I must catch up," he had said.

Chapter Twelve

A WEEK before Christmas it began to snow, and, much to the delight of the children, it went on and on like that. When it stopped, not only did everything look different outside, but all the usual things, like the baker's round and the post arriving at breakfast, were disrupted. It was a bad time for those who had plumbing, and those who had not shivered in their earth closets at the end of the garden and had to pour boiling water down the pumps every morning. Snow isn't such fun when you are grown-up. But children, in many ways so conservative (punctual meals, nothing strange to eat, "Who's that nasty man?"—the guest—and so on), are really little anarchists at heart. Quite out of hand, Mrs. Ethelburger's children put stones inside their snowballs and pelted their elders and betters. Ganging up with the village children (who in some ways had more original ideas), they shoved snow down the letter-box outside the post-office and stole trays which went down-hill much faster than the ordinary wooden toboggans. Mrs. Spark, coming out, muffled up to the eyes, with her fur coat and Wellingtons on, was attacked in her own drive and got her hat knocked off. But nothing could be done about it. Putting snow in the letter-box was serious, though.

"That is a criminal offence," Mr. Ethelburger told his children. "You could go to prison for that."

"You don't want to spend Christmas Day in prison, do you?" Mrs. Ethelburger said.

"Think of your poor mother and father," Mrs. Flint said.

They laid it on thick. But really, only the thaw could settle it. That came five days after Christmas.

Mr. Noyce had sent a copy of his book *More Stories for the Children*, which had come out some time previously, to Mrs. Ethelburger, inscribing it—"To comfort you, from H.N."

"Has he any nephews and nieces," Mr. Ethelburger said, "or why does he call himself 'Uncle Harry'? Queer chap."

As soon as the thaw made it possible, Mrs. Ethelburger went off to see Mr. Noyce. He was delighted. He gave her the big armchair so that she could curl up by the fire with a glass of brandy, and they talked for hours. It was dark before either of them noticed the time. The clock struck four.

"There!" Mrs. Ethelburger said.

"Oh, but, my dear Barbara, you're going to stay to tea!"

Mr. Noyce rang the bell. "Tea," he said when nurse came in.

"Hullo, Nurse, how have you been keeping?" Mrs. Ethelburger said.

"Oh, very well, thank you. And I hope all is well with you and your family down at the farm. What do you think of the Master? A shocking cold he had over Christmas, We thought it was the 'flu."

"But he looks marvellous!" Mrs. Ethelburger said. "There's nothing much wrong with him."

"Well, that's yourself," nurse said. "If I may say so, it does him good to have you visit us."

"Now come on, what about tea?" Mr. Noyce said. "You see," he said afterwards, "she's got me all to herself now that Eileen has gone. And she's pleased. Naughty of her."

"So are you," Mrs. Ethelburger said.

"Indeed, I'm not!"

"Yes, you are. It's what you always wanted."

"How can you say such a thing. It's just not true!"

"But you weren't awfully kind to her, were you?"

"Oh that!" Mr. Noyce said. "It wasn't a personal thing. I wanted her to get on with her painting."

"Well, she did. And she made a success of herself."

"*That's* not success," Mr. Noyce said.

"Well, it's one sort. After all, to be a success with the public, even if you are only a nine-days' wonder is the only sort of success most people count. You shouldn't be so difficult; you can't have things *exactly* as you want them."

"She's not going to get me to divorce her, though."

"Oh, that's wicked of you," Mrs. Ethelburger said. "No, Harry, you can't do that."

"Why not? How do you know, for instance, that I don't want her back?"

"Even if you did, it's not right. It's her life. Go on and do what she wants."

"Why should I? It's my life, too."

"No, it isn't. It may have been before. Now that she's made up her mind and is living with somebody else, she's nothing to do with you."

"That may be your idea. But it's certainly not the Law."

"But the Law isn't something above and outside. You men made it, you can damn well undo it," Mrs. Ethelburger said.

"You're getting quite excited. Isn't it bad for you, in your state? Anyway, don't let's quarrel. It reminds me of the bad old days."

"There you are, then! So you don't want her back. Look here, this was bound to happen the way you two went on. Why not be a help now you can't stop it, and make it really true?"

"Well, let's talk about something else. I'll think about it," Mr. Noyce said.

Mr. Ethelburger was a bit annoyed when his wife telephoned to ask him to come in the car and fetch her.

"You know, I can't do this often," he said as they drove home. "I've got work to do."

"I know," Mrs. Ethelburger said.

"I'm not a taxi."

"No, dear."

"Some people seem to think I am. This is the second time I've had to play the chauffeur to-day. Last time I was an ambulance. Mr. Browning had rather a nasty accident. I had to take him to hospital."

"Oh no!" Mrs. Ethelburger said. She put her hand up to her throat. "Was it bad?"

"Well, I don't know. He was rather a mess. Here we are. Jump out, will you? And I'll put the car away."

"Just a moment," Mrs. Ethelburger said.

"What's the matter? Oh dear, I forgot. Things like that upset women in your condition. So sorry. Shall I . . . Barbara!"

Mrs. Ethelburger fainted.

Confusion followed. Eventually she was got to bed, and Mrs. Flint was almost forcibly restrained from ringing up the doctor.

"Look here, I know what I'm talking about!" Mr. Ethelburger said. "She's perfectly all right now. Nothing's going to happen. She's over the dangerous months, and it's much too early for anything else. Come along, it's much more important for everybody's sake to shut those children up."

The children, all except the eldest who had taken this opportunity to snatch the papers and read about a rather horrible murder, were bawling their heads off.

Of course, Mr. Ethelburger put it all down to the fact that his wife had tired herself out with the visit to Mr. Noyce in the first place.

"Now you're not to do it again," he said that night when all was peace once more and everyone had gone to bed. "I'm sorry if I slipped up telling you about the accident. But really, it can't have been that, you know. You should be careful and not get so tired. No more visits to Mr. Noyce, please."

"Let's go to sleep," Mrs. Ethelburger said. He could tell from the tone of her voice that she wasn't going to take any notice whatsoever, and would probably, in the awkward spirit of defiance that marred her character, go off to the Manor next morning. Unless, perhaps, she didn't feel well enough.

He was wrong. Mrs. Ethelburger did not go to Mr. Noyce, she went to see Mrs. Browning. It proved to be a most unpleasant visit. Mrs. Browning would not even let her into the house, but kept her standing on the doorstep. And she refused to say anything at all about her son, not even which doctor he had or what the report from the hospital had been.

"But you must *know*," Mrs. Ethelburger said. Mrs. Browning slammed the door in her face. So Mrs. Ethelburger went back up the hill to the Rectory, and called in there to see if they knew. The Rector, very conscious of her condition, spoke in a reserved tone of voice, using many platitudes. Very alarmed, she hurried home and rang up the hospital. Mr. Browning was on the danger list, she was told. She mooned about for the rest of the day, followed by an anxious mother, and then, when she found herself alone, after dinner that evening, rang up the hospital again. To be told the same. She wasn't a relative, but with some persuasion they agreed to take her number and let her know should anything happen.

Next morning, when the telephone rang at about ten o'clock, she asked her mother to answer it. But it was Mr. Noyce. She went to speak to him.

"When are you coming to see me again?" he said.'

"Oh, could I come now?" she said.

"Funny, your voice sounds quite different over the phone. Yes, what about this afternoon?"

"But, my dear child, you are overdoing things, you are overdoing things!" Mrs. Flint said, when her daughter told her she might not be home till late that evening. "And what am I to say to John when he asks where you are at tea? You know what he is—"

"Oh, tell him I'm resting—anything," Mrs. Ethelburger said.

She arrived at the Manor, out of breath but looking very determined, at half-past two that afternoon. "Now look here," she said to Mr. Noyce, "you've got to help me. You are my friend, aren't you?"

"Why, yes," said Mr. Noyce, "of course."

"Well, then," Mrs. Ethelburger said, "order a taxi—you haven't got a car, have you? No. Well, then, order a taxi.

Mr. Browning has had an accident. It's absolutely vital that I see him. You see—oh, I really can't explain. Do help me!"

Mr. Noyce raised his eyebrows and made it clear he thought the whole thing very peculiar, but he did do what he had been asked to do. He was even prepared to go to the hospital in the taxi with Mrs. Ethelburger. But she said no, he was to stay at home, and if anyone asked where she was, he was to say she was there with him. When he protested about this, she said, "Oh, *please.*" And looked as though she might cry. So he said yes.

"But look, you are to come back here as soon as you possibly can," he said. "I don't say I shall require an explanation, but what on earth am I supposed to say to nurse, for instance? And cook has baked you a cake for tea. Oh, what a worry! I wouldn't do it for anyone else."

"You are a dear. I shall never forget this," Mrs. Ethelburger said.

"How very odd," Mr. Noyce said to himself, watching the taxi go off down the drive. Then he went and sat by the fire and lit a cigarette. Nurse knocked at the door and came in.

"Is anything the matter?" she said.

Mr. Noyce flicked the ash off his cigarette. "No. Why?" he said.

"But Miss Barbara and the taxi—I thought—"

"Miss Barbara—since when has it been Miss Barbara? Not very appropriate, Nurse, is it?"

"Well, where has she gone off to like that, then, Master Harry?"

Mr. Noyce raised his eyebrows again. "She'll be back soon. I shouldn't worry," he said. "As a matter of fact, it was my suggestion. You know what women are at these times. She told me she had a craving for pineapples. I happened to know where some are, so I sent her off in a taxi. An act of friendship. After all, she was very friendly with my father."

"But, Master Harry—you let her go alone like that?"

"Oh, that's carrying friendship a bit too far to expect me to go too," Mr. Noyce said. "After all, what would they think in the shop? . . . They might know one of us."

Nurse smiled and shook her head. "Dear Master Harry. And you look so stern, some people would never guess. But trust your old Nanny. She always knew," she said.

"Well, get on with you," said Mr. Noyce.

He read the paper for a bit. And then, pulling a crumpled envelope out of his pocket, took a note from inside it, and read that. "Give me ten shillings or I shall tell. You can send it," he read.

"I suppose really, it's a matter for the police," he said to himself. "And yet, one doesn't like to. Silly child. I wish that woman would come back. What the hell's she been up to, I wonder?" He looked at the clock.

It was four o'clock by the time she came back. Mr. Noyce told the taxi-man to wait while they had tea. "I'm not going to let you walk home. And it will save your husband," he said.

Mrs. Ethelburger seemed very excited and talked a lot, and ate very little tea. He let her talk. She offered no explanation about her conduct, and he did not ask. At last, just before it was time for her to go, he showed her the note. "I rather wanted your advice about this," he said. "It's Linda, you know. The little village girl who used to work here. The one who caused rather a lot of trouble. I suppose, you know who I mean?"

"Oh yes, I know," said Mrs. Ethelburger. "She's walking out now with one of the boys from the factory. Not a very nice young man. He's at the awkward age. Pimples. What does she know about to tell?"

"Of course, nothing," Mr. Noyce said. "Silly of you to ask that, don't you think, when I might ask you quite a lot of things? But just as there is nothing in this, in your case there is nothing queer either, I'm sure."

"Well, do you know what I'd do? I'd take that note to her father, show it to him and then say, 'Any more nonsense and I go to the police.' Then put it back in your pocket and march out."

Soon after this Mrs. Ethelburger put on her coat and got ready to say good-bye. "It's not much good my saying thank you," she said before going into the hall; "but it's one of the nicest things that has ever happened to me, you doing what you did. And only you could have done it that way. One day I'll tell you all about it; if we really are going to be friends, that is."

"But we are friends—it seems to me we are," Mr. Noyce said.

"Ah, but it takes time, friendship. It takes a long time to grow. Perhaps you'll come and see me sometimes?"

"Now, that would be a test," Mr. Noyce said. "I can't bear children—it's as much as I can do to write for them!"

"There you are, you see. Well, I shan't be able to come over here much more, not till after the baby. So if you want us to be friends, you'd better come and see me."

"Absence makes the heart grow fonder, you know," Mr. Noyce said.

Nurse knocked at the door. "The taxi is ready- waiting," she said.

"Good-bye, Nurse," Mrs. Ethelburger said, going out into the hall. "And please will you thank Mrs. Walmby very much for the cake. It was lovely."

"I shall tell her," nurse said. "And I hope you got your pineapple all right, Miss Barbara."

"*Not* Miss Barbara!" Mr. Noyce said. "Come along, into your taxi—just think how it's been charging up!" He took Mrs. Ethelburger by the arm and jostled her away.

"Pineapple?" she said.

"Here's the fare. You won't have enough money. Women never have. I'll explain the pineapple in the years to come, when we have become friends at last and you explain," Mr. Noyce said.

He did go to the farm to see her. But only once, quite soon after this, when the Rector rang him up and told him that Mr. Browning had died. He told himself it was not curiosity that made him go, and yet there seemed no other explanation for a visit at this time. So he went to the Darlingtons' first (killing two birds with one stone as it were, and, besides, giving him a chance to say he had just dropped in, finding himself in the vicinity).

"Now don't whip her, Darlington," he said. "That's not the thing. Can't you find out why she behaves like this?"

They sat on the horsehair sofa in that cold little parlour, where months ago Mrs. Spark had interviewed Mrs. Darlington about her daughter. Nothing at all was altered in that room. But perhaps it was colder.

"She's flighty and pert, that's what she is," Mr. Darlington said, "and wants it all her own way. I don't know what's to become of her."

"They're like that, aren't they, women?" Mr. Noyce said.

Mr. Darlington looked the other way.

"Oh, it's all right. I suppose everyone knows now, do they?"

"A lot of tittle-tattle," Mr. Darlington said uneasily.

"Tittle-tattle is generally right," Mr. Noyce said, and then remembering the purpose of his visit, "but, of course, when people get hold of the wrong end of the stick—no, gossip and things like that are always an evil."

"You must do as you think fit, Sir," Mr. Darlington said.

"Well, any more nonsense and I go to the police!"

"She's going to be married."

"To the pi—to the factory man?"

"Yes, that's him. Who's been telling you that, if I may ask, Sir? We've never favoured him much, the wife and I. And I wouldn't have told you myself, if it hadn't been for, well—what you said like about the police."

"Oh, how does one get to know these things?"

"That's just it, Sir. Still, you may as well know the whole thing. She's got to. That's what it is."

"Oh, I see," Mr. Noyce said. "Well, then, perhaps it's only fair to tear this up."

"We are ashamed. That's what we are. She's brought nothing but shame on us."

"Don't take it like that. She'll learn."

"That she never will. Haven't I tried all these years? And it's been no good. I should have stuck to the roses. Yes, I should."

"I was sorry when you left."

"Ah, it was too late then."

"Well, cheer up, she'll soon be off your hands!"

"It's a terrible thing when a man wishes his own child hadn't been born. And I do that," Mr. Darlington said.

The interview ended soon afterwards. However, Mr. Noyce did not tear the note up, just in case. "Fear thy God," he said, going away up the path. "What an awful thing to have on a plate! He always was a gloomy sort of chap."

He found Mrs. Ethelburger in good health. Nothing at all was said about Mr. Browning, except at tea (which they had together with Mr. Ethelburger, the children having theirs apart with Mrs. Flint), when Mr. Ethelburger said, "Very sad about Mr. Browning."

"So sad for his mother," Mrs. Ethelburger said.

Much later on, one day when nurse brought in his cup of tea in the middle of the morning, the subject of Mr. Browning cropped up again. Nurse had met the Rector on one of her rare visits to the village. He had been there at the end, nurse said. "It was a happy release," she added. "And he died happy. Ever so happy, the Rector said."

"Well, it's always nice to know that," Mr. Noyce said.

"And the old woman's gone to live with her sister; so we'll doubtless have strangers in the village sooner or later."

"That reminds me, heard anything of Mrs. Ethel-burger—anything happened yet?" Mr. Noyce said.

"It isn't time yet," nurse said.

"Funny how you women always know that sort of thing."

"It's a very important thing, Master Harry."

"Oh, quite. Well, when you hear, let me know."

"But of course I shall," nurse said.

It took Mr. Noyce a long time to make up his mind about divorcing his wife. But just like him, he woke up one morning and found that it had all been decided for him in his head while he slept. He thought, of course, it was a simple matter. He wrote to his solicitors, enclosing the hotel bill. But it wasn't so easy as that. The hotel bill was much too old, the solicitors wrote back. It meant starting again from the beginning. Mr. Noyce was suddenly struck with fear that his wife might have got tired of her lover, or something had happened to stop her wanting a divorce. And besides, there was collusion. But all was arranged in time. However, it meant visits to London. One way and another, Mr. Noyce was kept busy, so he only found time to write a short note to Mrs. Ethelburger to congratulate her on the birth of her baby—another son.

"So nice of you to write," she wrote back, "and I'm terribly glad to hear about the divorce. You know, I dreamed it. I dreamed I saw a ship sailing all alone on the waters of the sea. No one steered it, no one was on it, but the sails were blowing out in the wind and a seagull always flew before it. I stood on the shore at the edge of the waves, and someone was standing beside me. 'Where is the ship going?' I said. 'No one knows,' he said, 'but unless it is set free, it will be dashed to pieces on the rocks.' I looked and saw that this was true. Nearer and nearer it was leaning to the shore with the seagull always before. 'But it must be saved,' I said. 'No one can save it,' the stranger said, 'it is not free.' And then suddenly the seagull lifted himself up on his wings and turned into the wind and flew away. And the ship, like someone waking, righted itself and went out to sea."

"Strange," Mr. Noyce said, smiling over this letter. "I don't see why she should connect it with my affairs, though. More likely something has happened to herself. Having that baby. Women are strange."

It wasn't till after the divorce, when Mrs. Ethelburger's baby was four months old, that they met again.

"Hullo, stranger," Mr. Noyce said.

"Oh, don't say that!" Mrs. Ethelburger said.

"About that peculiar business last time you were here," Mr. Noyce said after tea. "Or is it too early on in our friendship to talk about that?"

"Yes," Mrs. Ethelburger said. "It's going to be rather too drawn out otherwise, perhaps. But the pineapple, you tell me about that first."

Mr. Noyce explained about the pineapple. "Now it's your turn," he said.

"Well, look. Mine's rather more serious. In fact, you've got to promise never to tell," she said.

"Oh, we won't speak about it at all, if you'd rather not," Mr. Noyce said.

Mrs. Ethelburger sighed. "The thing is, I hate secrets really," she said. "They eat one away inside. So if I tell you, it won't be a secret any more. I know that is selfish. But I can't bear it. You see, it was Lawrence—Mr. Browning's child. I couldn't let him die without telling him that."

Mr. Noyce stared into the fire and sighed a bit. "Yes," he said. "Yes. It was quite brave of you really. What on earth would you have done, though, if the fellow had lived?"

"Well, I had to risk that, didn't I? After all, one human being to another—I couldn't let him go off into nothing leaving nothing. What's a woman for? No, any woman would tell you, I had to do that."

CHAPTER THIRTEEN

THAT perhaps should be the end of the story. But it would leave a false impression to end like that. For instance, the character of this little village which changed noticeably at the death of old Mr. Noyce, changes so swiftly during the next few years that by the time Harry Noyce sells up the last of his property and the Manor-house becomes a preparatory school for boys, the village is a village no longer. As a suburb of the town, it has an improved bus service (one every hour instead of two a day), a new factory, twenty new Council houses and a steady amount of building on one-acre plots, and a new post-office and several new shops. A lot of sighing goes on over the brown teapots, and some of the farmers make a row when strangers come and dig the fields up and lay down enormous pipes for main drainage. But they were the ones who made the fuss about electricity and telephones; and if they are still alive, they will carry on about television (a television aerial is vaguely reminiscent of the devil's pitchfork, I think they would notice that).

But Mrs. Spark catches something of the right spirit when she says, "Back to the land with the dynamos over our heads!" Which doesn't sound queer if you are frightfully excited and say it a lot. The new people in the new houses rather like Mrs. Spark. They like her being eccentric, marching about with her grey stick with the silver band at the top, looking firm. "An indomitable old lady," the local paper calls her when she tries to break up a Conservative meeting at election time. They do not take her politics seriously; but she *is* an old lady, and there is something fine about living so long, and they are grateful to her for calling attention to it.

The Rector is not very popular. In fact, if it had not been for his wife, there would have been agitation for a new man at the Rectory; someone younger, abreast of the times. It seems to quite a lot of people that a big old house like that, with all that garden, taking up so much space where space is valuable for housing, is shockingly wasted on an old man with no family who isn't really interested in what goes on around him. For nowadays the Rector spends a good deal of time reading the *Meditations of Marcus Aurelius* in the boathouse at the bottom of the garden. People may not know this, but his lack of enthusiasm when approached about Sunday cinema shows for the children is too obvious; so that they feel the kindest thing to do is to write the poor old man off as a back-number, like the folk in the Almshouses—whom it's kind to say "Good morning" to, but doesn't do to visit.

Mr. Ethelburger sometimes speaks about "giving up the farm." But he doesn't really mean it. In some ways he takes absolutely no notice of the change which has occurred. He goes to church, sitting in the same place in the same pew; he goes to the same old pub, even when they build a new one much nearer him, and talks, as far as possible, to the same old people. On the other hand, he goes in for a model dairy with all the very latest equipment. He is prosperous. His children are all having the best education that money can buy, because, as he says, "The Public Schools still count."

"How?" Mrs. Ethelburger says.

But nowadays she is not nearly such a nuisance. She had no more children after her fifth. She spoils this one. The other four, spending eight months of the year away, are strangers. And she never liked them much; but Stevie, the last, is her own, her baby. She settles down to worry about him, to cherish him, to live for him. He is delicate.

A few years of this, and she looks old. Parting from her, Mr. Noyce is much more relieved than distressed. Her conversation has become so dull.

"Honestly, what do you think he did to-day? Climbed out of the nursery window, down the drain-pipe! I had to get the ladder out to rescue him from over the porch."

"Really."

"Oh, but, Harry—he is such fun—how can I explain?"

"My dear, don't look so anxious, you don't have to."

"But I want you to understand."

"Barbara, you have changed."

"But of course I have changed! It's this little chap. He gets round me. 'Are you smiling?' he says when I'm cross with him, and of course I smile. You couldn't help loving him for that."

"Charming. But you need a rest from it, though. Tell me about yourself. Or what about me? Or Eileen. Do you remember Eileen?"

"Yes, of course. It was so sad you and she never had any children. And she wanted them, too. But she's got them now. Let's see, how old would hers be? Six months younger than mine, I think. Six months is like years in a small child's life. Do you know, I really can't remember what Stevie was like six months ago? Give me Eileen's address, and I'll write. What fun if the two little boys could meet!"

"My dear, *can't* we stop talking about brats?"

"Yes, they *are* brats, aren't they? Cruel little things. Perhaps that's why one loves them so much. And so innocent in a frightening way. Do you know what he said when he asked and I told him about God? He said—"

"Oh, Barbara. This is the end. If we are going to talk about the Almighty, do let us be adult."

"But it *is* adult, in a way. That's just what I was going to tell you. Never mind. Dear Harry, don't be cross. The last thing I want to do is to bore you."

But she did.

In the brief intervals from his distress at having to leave his home (a question of finance, now or never is the time to sell up, and with a good offer, he chooses now). Mr. Noyce shuts himself in his study to write.

"June 29th. High Summer," he writes, "the gay time of the year when the flowers are out. But we are old, our thoughts have dug in. We do not blossom but pursue growth underground; blanched and hidden, alone, blind. Perhaps it was always that way. Friend answers to friend, not knowing the other, but guessing the distance between them that compels them to love. We have what we needed.

It is necessary for me to be a wanderer. To be most myself I should be always searching, sometimes finding, never settled. For her the opposite. She lacked the child, her lover's child, and having found him is completed. It is not the distance that matters—how much farther could we be apart, a man and a woman—it is the narrow lines we allow for our lives to be lived in. Damming up the main stream, we compel the water forward so that the banks and fields on either side are no longer fertilised and the tributaries dispersed. All this for the sake of some great reservoir that we imagine. Or perhaps we hope that somehow, some-where, we shall find the sea. The sea is the mother, they say. What slippery creatures we were when we climbed out of it! And what dry old bones we shall be when it laps us in!"

He writes no more stories for the children. And nurse has grown so old that her mind wanders. Mrs. Walmby, herself ripe with old age, treats her with respect, bring-ing her cups of tea and saying, "Yes, there now, and so it was when I come to think of it," when she fails to under-stand what old nurse says. Mrs. Walmby is going to live in one of the Almshouses. It is all settled; she looks forward to buying new curtains with her savings. She wants new spectacles, and a wireless, and time to herself. Nothing else. It is a bit more difficult about nurse.

"You understand, we are leaving here," Mr. Noyce says, leaning on the mantelpiece, warming himself by the fire.

"Yes," nurse says, "a good holiday is what you need, Master Harry. I've always said."

"But we are not coming back."

"Now, don't you distress yourself. Don't be so impatient. It will come out all right in the end. It will, I know it will, Master Harry. You should have faith, like me."

The day comes when the men come to take the furniture away. Mr. Noyce has bought a new house in London, though he does not feel like settling down.

"A *pied-à-terre*," he tells Mrs. Ethelburger. "Nurse will be able to look after it while I'm away. And of course Lettice will be there. She's so glad to have a home, you know. Funny to think of us coming together. Marianne lives quite near, only a few streets away. It'll be like when we were children. Only I shan't very often be there. Travel. That's the thing. It doesn't do for a person like me to be cooped up like poultry."

Suddenly he notices Mrs. Ethelburger is crying. It irritates him.

"Oh, I know it's the right thing to weep," he says. "It's terribly sad, I know. But don't let us be sentimental. I am going while the going is good, that's all. I could have hung on. Perhaps if I died during the next twelve years, the money would have lasted. But isn't that rather a melancholy way?"

"But you belonged here. You belong," Mrs. Ethelburger said.

"I know, that's what I used to say. But I was being sentimental. It hasn't worked out like that. One must go on."

"Why?"

"Oh, really! Let's go. I'm tired of walking about. I'm tired of this place. In another minute I shall feel miserable at leaving it all, just as you want me to."

They were walking by the lake. And now, turning their backs on it, they went up a narrow path towards the house.

"It'll be a swimming-pool, that's what it'll be," Mr. Noyce said, "a nice swimming-pool for the boys. I hope they drown themselves. Now look what you've made me say!"

"And what will happen to the swan?" Mrs. Ethelburger said.

"Lock, stock and barrel, it's sold with the place. I suppose it will go on boring itself to death, disenchanted. Those boys will make a fearful noise splashing about, won't they? But I dare say they'll have it 'put away.' Difficult to catch, though."

They turned round to have a look.

"One of the masters will shoot it. The gym instructor."

"He'll miss," said Mrs. Ethelburger, "and the swan will rise up on its wings and fly away."

"Dear Barbara. Do you remember that time you came here and I startled you so? Do you remember?"

She has succeeded in making him feel sad, which is what he ought to feel. He won't regret it later, it will add charm to his memories, help to eke out the splendour of the past, to fix in a sunset mood the background of his later days.

All nurse said when the furniture removers came in and she tottered off on Mr. Noyce's arm was "Punishment."

"Punishment?" Mr. Noyce said. "But we're going to have a much better time in London, Nurse. You and I and Miss Lettice. Just like old times for you it'll be. You should have gone before, as I told you to. But you would stay. Now, come along."

Mrs. Ethelburger waves to them from the steps of the house as they go off in the car to the station. She is standing by to keep an eye on things—her own idea—Mr. Noyce has a perfectly competent agent. Mr. Broom is there too. He watches the car go down the drive, and then says to Mrs. Ethelburger, with the hint of a smile on his face:

"Well, we must be getting on."

They want him for an odd-job man at the school. He knows the place, he will be quite useful. (They don't know, though, what a fuss he will make when they start cutting trees down.)

Stevie, Mrs. Ethelburger's son, pulls at her arm. "Coming," she says, "just a moment, dear."

He pulls again.

"Don't," she says.

He pulls harder.

"All right, Stevie, all right, dear," she says.

She allows him to lead her, and they walk away.

THE END

FURROWED MIDDLEBROW

Printed in Great Britain
by Amazon

50134798R00112